Mrs. Daniel

Reaping the Whirlwind

A Novel: Vol. II.

Mrs. Daniel

Reaping the Whirlwind
A Novel: Vol. II.

ISBN/EAN: 9783337067236

Printed in Europe, USA, Canada, Australia, Japan

Cover: Foto ©Andreas Hilbeck / pixelio.de

More available books at **www.hansebooks.com**

REAPING THE WHIRLWIND.

A NOVEL.

IN THREE VOLUMES.

BY

MRS. MACKENZIE DANIEL,

Author of "After Long Years," "Miriam's Sorrow," "My Sister Minnie," "Our Guardian," &c.

VOL. II.

London:

T. CAUTLEY NEWBY, PUBLISHER,

30, WELBECK STREET, CAVENDISH SQUARE.

1864.

REAPING THE WHIRLWIND.

CHAPTER I.

BLABBERTY CUETSUMS.

" LAWKS, miss, whatever has kept you out so late? Here's Missis getting into a pretty flurry about you, and me and Miss Gertrude has been ever so far down the road to see if you was in sight. Such a pity too, as you was out this evening, for there's been the handsomest and the pleasantest spoken gentleman a calling here as ever you see. I happened

to be standing at the gate just for a breath of
air, as I may be doing now; well, up he
comes, and asks with such a free smile
and in such a polite voice, if this was called
Lindenhurst. 'Yes, it is, sir,' I says to him,
thinking to myself, 'I wonder who you
are,' 'and the lady,' I says, 'who lives here is
Mrs. Beamish, and if you want to speak to
her she's at home with the oldest of the young
ladies; the other one, Miss Ethel,' I says,
'sir, being gone out for a walk this fine evening, leastways not exactly for a walk, but to
make enquiries about a poor lady in the village, who was took very bad last night, sir,
after the feet at Beechwood;' and then, miss,
he smiled so pleasant, and said he would come
in, and he sent me with a card to Missis, and
I fetched him into the drawing-room, and he
stayed above an hour; and after that, Miss
Gertrude showed him all round the garden,
which, as I was a passing the drawing-room
door accidental, I heerd him say he wanted
particular to see, though by the looks of him,

Miss, I should guess he comes from a much finer place than ours. And then, as he was a going away at last, and I stood holding open the gate to him, he says, 'good night, Mary,' in such a free and haffable manner, and with the beautifullest of smiles, that I was quite taken aback, and hadn't even the sense to tell him my name wasn't Mary; but to be sure, miss, it didn't matter what he called me. I only wish you'd been at home, for it's not often that such as this gentleman who's been here to-night comes our way."

As the whole of the above was given in one breath, with a total contempt for stops of any kind, and with the speaker's mouth foaming from her vehemence, I had no choice but to listen to the end. At the first pause, I said—

" Betsy, if there was the least chance of any other family in England putting up with your incorrigible tongue, I would induce mamma to give you warning to-morrow. I cannot stay to talk to you about your folly now ; but we must either cure you of it soon,

or prevent your ever seeing strangers. Where
shall I find mamma and Miss Gertrude?"

" They was just gone back to the drawing
room, Miss, when I come out.   I'm very sorry,
I'm sure, that my tongue should run away with
me, Miss Ethel, as you say it does, and I
can't deny but what I've been called a great
chatter-box before now—indeed grandmother,
poor dear old soul! who's gone to Heaven
a year come next Christmas, used to say I'd
talk a cat's hind leg off."

Without staying to offer any comment upon
this remarkable prophesy, I hastened to show
myself indoors, and to convince mamma that
nobody had been insane enouge to run away
with her precious daughter.

"Surely," I said, (when, as is usual in these
cases,) they were repeating for the second or
third time their wonderings and surmises as
to my long absence—" Surely Mr. Kenyon
must have mentioned the time at which he
met me at the stepping stones, and this ought
to have shown you that I had loitered and

even strayed out of my road in going to the village. I could not have possibly done the latter half of my journey faster than I did; indeed I ran nearly all the way home."

"That was foolish," said mamma, drawing me nearer the lamp to see if I was much heated—"but, Ethel, Mr. Kenyon never mentioned having met you at all—did he Gertie?"

"No, I am sure he did not," my sister answered—"for I was wondering how it was he omitted enquiring after you in any way, and of course I should have understood it had he alluded to this meeting. How very odd of him."

"Not particularly odd, either," I said, a little indignant nevertheless. "I suppose he considered the circumstance too trivial to be worth mentioning. How did you like him, mamma?"

"Well, I was really excessively pleased with him;" my mother replied quite warmly. "He and I had a long talk together before your sister joined us. I found him not only full of information on general subjects, but apparently deeply interested in the one most young men shrink from or speak lightly of. It was he, not I, who introduced religion into our conversation, but I must say I have rarely discussed it with a more earnest, humble-minded and apparently sincere admirer of its doctrines and precepts. I told him he ought to have been a clergyman."

"And what did you think of him, Gertie?" I asked, turning suddenly to my sister, who was busy with some needlework.

"You put this same question to me yesterday, Ethel, if you remember," said the stitcher, looking up for a moment with her quiet smile. "I can still only answer as I did then, that he seemed agreeable and gentle-manly. Except that mamma admires him so much, I don't know that there is any need for our forming opinions about Mr. Kenyon at all. We are not likely to become intimate with him."

"Oh, by the bye, what about Mrs. Vivian's gracious invitation. Is it to be accepted?"

"Why, yes," mamma answered. "I didn't see how we could reasonably or politely refuse it, especially as the offer of the carriage removed every difficulty. Gertie is not enchanted at the prospect, but I hope when once you are there, you will both enjoy it."

"I detest parties," Gertie said drawing her thread out with a jerk, which I quite understood as indicative of irritation, "and assuredly had it been left to me, I should have declined this one without a moment's hesitation. The very idea of schoolmistresses dressing up and going to dancing parties like idle, flirting girls, is to me ridiculous in the extreme. I hope nobody else will ever invite us."

"I don't quite agree with you in this, my dear," said mamma gently. "While you are young and happy there can be no reason in the world against your mingling in any innocent gaiety, which other young and happy women enjoy. I am sure if I thought the occupation that has been chosen for you (here the fond mother's voice became a little tremulous) was to disqualify you for the ordinary amusements befitting your age and station, I would rather add to our income by taking in washing, or go and live in the smallest and cheapest cottage in England, than let my dear girls be schoolmistresses."

"Mamma," said Gertrude, very gravely and earnestly, "believe me, once for all, when I assure you that I would rather be what I am, or rather what I hope to be, than the richest, the idlest, the most prosperous lady in the land. If my taste is an uncommon one, it is none the less real. Ethel can do as she likes about mingling the usual recreations of youth with her life's work. There is nothing wrong in it to those who can conscientiously unite the two. I don't think *I* could, so I only hope our kind friends and neighbours will leave me in peace."

As soon as I could get my sister alone, I

enquired what she had accomplished with mamma on the subject—becoming a somewhat vexed one by this time—of Guy and Meta.

"I am utterly bewildered at mamma's persistency and infatuation," she said, a little wearily; and then I knew that this matter had ruffled her temper also. "She refuses to hear anything against Meta, has every excuse to offer for her love of admiration, and winds up by begging me to think as kindly and indulgently as I can of one who will certainly be our brother's wife some day."

"Poor mamma! she believes so fully that Guy's life or reason would desert him were it otherwise that she will not even glance at the possibility of Meta's eventually refusing him. I warned you how small a measure of success to expect, Gertie. You see I have watched this little matter for some time."

"It is far from a little matter," sighed my sister, as she folded up her work for the evening—"but I am tired of thinking about it now, Ethel. Will you have one turn before supper in the gardens to see what stars are visible. On bright summer nights like these, we must bring the children out and teach them the elements of astronomy."

It seemed clear that from all the minor vexations and annoyances of her daily life, Gertrude would turn for consolation to the profession which was (at any rate in anticipation) hope and joy, and an all satisfying interest to her.

The next day my sister went early to the village, both to gain tidings of Miss Dora and to convey to Jane Norton, as she had undertaken to do, Mrs Vivian's invitation for the following Monday. She found the invalid rather better, but still too weak and nervous to see any body except her sister and the doctor. Miss Downing appeared pleased that her niece should have been thought of by the great lady of Fell House, and it was settled that Jane should spend the afternoon of Monday at Lindenhurst, go with us to the party, and sleep at our house that night.

"Oh, and I met the vicar as I was coming away," said Gertie, when she had told me all the above. "He was bringing a basket of apricots to Miss Dora, the first ripe ones that had been gathered this season, he told me, and I wondered whether they were from those standard trees which used to produce such a splendid crop in our time. By the bye, he asked particularly after you, Ethel, and said I was to tell you Maggie was very busy getting her little stock of books ready. I think you are a favourite with the vicar."

"He is always very kind and friendly to me; but you see he looks on me now, not as Ethel Beamish, but as Margaret Wyke's teacher, and hence any interest out of the common which he may feel in me."

"Well, that is natural enough. I hope Maggie will get on with us, but she is such a shy, unapproachable little thing, that I am afraid it will not be very easy to teach her amongst others. I wonder in her case Mr.

Wyke should not have preferred a governess at home."

"I suppose being a widower, he could only have had an elderly lady to reside in the house, and Maggie does not like elderly ladies at all."

"Poor child! then if her father should marry again, she won't be very fond of her step-mother, I am afraid."

I laughed as I enquired why not. Did Gertie know of any vow Mr. Wyke was under to marry none but an elderly lady.

"He is almost too old himself to marry a young one," my sister said, in the rather positive way which was natural to her. "Mr. Wyke must be forty at the least, and of course he would not choose a wife under thirty. It would be ridiculous, especially in a clergyman."

"I cannot see that at all," I answered, as positively this time as my sister. "Why, when he first came here, some of us were thinking of Alicia Clarkson for him, and nobody ever suggested that such a match would be absurd."

"What a set of gossips and match-makers you all are at Graybourne," said Gertrude, laughing now, but mingling a little disdain with her laugh. "I gave you credit for more sense, Ethel, but I suppose two months of village society is enough to inoculate any one with the disease always raging in villages."

"One must have some amusement, you know," I said, "and theoretical match-making at women's tea parties is at least more innocent and blameless than back-biting and scandal. I don't think we are much given to these dangerous vices at Graybourne. Mrs. Arnott might be, but we are, upon the whole, a virtuous little community, take my word for it, Gertie; and you must not, in your superior wisdom, be too hard upon us."

"I am only trembling lest I should catch the disease, too," laughed my sister, as Betsy appeared to summon us to dinner; "so mind

you watch me well, Ethel, and sound a
friendly note of warning when the first
dangerous symptom appears."

The next day was Sunday, and after the
morning service Gertie and myself went
round to call on the Downings, none of their
household having been at church. We found
Miss Harriet quite knocked up from her close
attendance upon her sister, and Jane Norton
acting as nurse to them both. The latter,
however, who seemed rather to enjoy her
novel duties, took the first opportunity of
telling me that Mr. Burns had been to see
them the day before, that he had brought a
large parcel of books for aunt Harriet, and,
better still, a delicious little dormouse for
herself.

" You know I told him the other day how
fond I was of dormice, and that I had not
had one for years, but of course I never
thought for a moment that he would give me
such a thing. I must show it you, Miss
Ethel—it is the greatest beauty you ever saw

in your life, and so soft, I am wanting to be stroking him all day. I have named it 'Blabberty Cuetsums'—do you think it a pretty name?"

"An uncommon one, undoubtedly, Jane, and I should imagine requiring some ingenuity in its invention. Did it take you long?"

"Oh dear no; I thought of it almost at once—but wasn't it kind of Mr. Burns to bring me such a nice present? I do like him so much."

"I suppose he only paid you a short visit yesterday?"

"No—he would not stay ten minutes when he heard of aunt Dora's illness, but he is to come to tea one evening next week."

Both Gertie and myself offered to remain at the cottage for the afternoon if we could be of any use to the sick inmates, but Miss Downing would not hear of our giving up our Sunday, and was quite sure she should be strong and well again by the evening. Jane had proved herself a very skilful little nurse, and could continue doing for them all that was required.

" And about to-morrow evening ?" I asked, really anxious that poor Jane should not be disappointed of her party at the Vivian's. " If you are not better, Miss Harriet, may I take your niece's place for a few hours while she is at Fell House.   The entertainment will probably be more in her way than ours."

" Oh," said Gertrude eagerly—" you know how I want to get out of this tiresome party, Ethel.   If Miss Downing will accept either of us in lieu of Jane, do let it be me."

" My dears, it shall be neither of you," replied Miss Downing positively.   " I shall be quite myself after a night's rest, and even were it to be otherwise I would not detain that poor child at home for the world."

So it was no use urging the matter further, and after a peep at Jane's dormouse, and a few more ecstasies on that young lady's part

concerning both it and its donor, we said good
bye and went home by the meadow road I
had taken two nights ago when the dreaming
fit had come upon me.

CHAPTER II.

TWILIGHT AND THE VICAR.

I STRUGGLED the whole of Monday morning against a desperate headache which had attacked me on getting out of bed, and continued to grow worse and worse with every remedy I tried to subdue it. Nevertheless, as I knew how seriously annoyed Gertrude would be if she had to go to the Vivians without me, I would not entirely give up hope of conquering the enemy, or even acknowledge how sick and helpless I really felt, until Jane Norton arrived in the afternoon. By this time I was suffering intensely, and on

Jane's exclaiming how pale I looked, I found
sudden courage to say to my sister : —

"Gertie, it is no good. I have done my
best, but you see it is all useless. The pain
is becoming sharper every minute, and I
must abandon all idea of the party, and go
to bed instead."

I believe I have hinted before that if this
dear sister of mine had a fault visible to those
around her, it was a little quickness of temper,
on what often appeared to me and others very
slight occasions. As I spoke now, she looked
up abruptly from her work ; her face flushed,
her brow contracted, and she said, in rather a
hard tone, at least it sounded hard to me,
with my poor head throbbing as it did : —

"I never knew anything so provoking and
unfortunate in my life, Ethel. Strange that
you, who don't get a headache once in six
months, should get one for this particular
evening."

"Dear," I replied, wearily (I was too ill
to be indignant), "you don't, I hope, ques-

tion its reality. Even if I were hypocrite enough to feign illness at any time, the motive would be lacking in this case. I rather liked the idea of going to Fell House than otherwise."

"More than I do," retorted Gertrude, still in the same pitiless voice, "if your headache were a hundred times worse than it is, and would leave you for me, I should only be too thankful."

With this she gathered up her work, and, not condescending to bestow another glance upon me, walked, in a dignified manner, out of the parlour.

And I, finding mamma, and gaining abundance of sympathy and kind words from her, went dejectedly to my own room, asking Jane, who I saw was burning with indignation against my sister, to bring me a cup of tea when the family had theirs at five o'clock.

Soon after getting into bed I fell asleep, and was awakened two hours later by the pressure of a soft, cool hand upon my fore-

head. I started up with a vague impression
that it must be Jane Norton who had come
to bring me my tea, but instead of Jane, my
sister stood beside me, no longer angry or
doubting, but kind, gentle, affectionate, as
was her wont to be.

"Are you better, dear? has your sleep
refreshed you? Will you have some tea now,
or shall I bathe your forehead a little first?
Poor Ethel—I wish I could bear the pain for
you."

And I was sure she did, quite apart now
from a desire to escape going to the Vivians.
Gertie's irritation never lasted long, and
though she was not in the habit of acknowledging her fault in words, being of a reserved
and very proud nature, she always showed
by her manner that she was sincerely grieved
on account of it, and willing to make any
atonement in her power.

"I will have some tea, Gertie, please," I
replied, holding out my hand to her, " my
head is still aching miserably, but I am better

here than down stairs. Let me see both yourself and Jane when you are dressed, will you?"

"Certainly, dear child. We must begin that unpleasant business, I suppose, as soon as tea is over."

I thought her looking very lovely when at length she came and stood in her pure white dress at the foot of my bed and enquired laughingly (she was determined to show no more naughty tempers on the subject of the party) whether she should " do."

Encouraged by her apparent cheerfulness, and in good spirits from feeling a little easier since tea, I replied jestingly:—

"You do so beautifully, Gertie, that I am afraid somebody's heart will be quite done for to-night. Mr. Walter Kenyon may have remained invulnerable hitherto, but—"

I was warned in time. I saw the red mounting into her cheek, the frown gathering on her smooth, white brow. How stupid of me to forget that my sister's tastes had

ever been violently opposed to every species
of jesting on these kind of topics. Still, I
should have expected only a little impatient
shrug of the shoulders, not the anger which,
had I finished my foolish speech, it would
certainly have provoked. Poor dear Gertie!
she had been put out so much already to-day.

As I paused abruptly, and bit my lips to
keep them quiet, Gertie stooped down and
kissed me.

" Good night, Ethel dear. Try to go to
sleep again, and to be quite well by the morning. Jane shall sleep with me for fear of
disturbing you."

Then Jane came in, fresh from mamma's
and Betsy's hands, and looking very nice and
attractive too. She promised me a full,
genuine, and particular account of the party
and everybody at it, expressed a thousand
regrets at my being obliged to stay at home,
kissed and wished me good night, and followed
Gertrude down stairs.

Then a few minutes later came the carriage

from Fell House and took them away, the willing and the unwilling guest, to the scene of gaiety.

It was still early (for Mrs. Vivian's party being ostensibly a juvenile one, she had chosen a very moderate hour for the assembling of her friends), and when mamma came up to me on the departure of my sister and her companion, I said I would dress myself in a loose wrapper, and get down to the sofa in the drawing-room.

" Do, dear," mamma replied, " for it is a cool, lovely evening, and I think you will enjoy lying by the open window and breathing the fresh air. I shall be busy with Betsy for another hour or so, as she is going to make some jam to-night, but with your headache you will perhaps be better alone."

To which I assented, and, refusing mamma's offer of assistance, quickly slipped on a dressing gown, and went down to the sofa and the open window, and the delicious quiet of our large, cool drawing-room.

Here, as was natural, the sweet spirit of sleep very soon came and breathed a gentle blessing over me again. Languid both from the pain I had endured, and the influence of the soft summer air, I could not keep awake, and I did not care to do so. They are generally pleasant dreams that visit us in the snatches of sleep into which we are lulled by stillness and a July atmosphere. I dreamt now of green, shady forests and babbling streams, and wild flowers that were springing up thickly and luxuriantly beneath my feet; and then suddenly, in the very centre of the fair, smiling scene, in which I had been revelling alone, appeared a dark, stagnant lake, and by this lake sat a woman with her head bowed down between her hands, apparently weeping. I went up to her and asked her why she cried; I touched her on the shoulder and she seemed to quiver under my touch. "Who are you," I said—" and what is this lake by which you sit and weep so bitterly?" Then a voice I did not know, answered—" I

weep for the lake which was once clear and
bright and flowing, but has been poisoned
and made dark and stagnant as you see—it
was done in wantonness, in sport, and in reck-
lessness of what might be the result, but it
is done for ever." With these last words,
uttered in an indescribably pathetic tone,
which seemed to wring my own heart, and
brought tears to my own eyes, the speaker
looked round at me slowly, and revealed to
my horror, rather than to my surprise or
mystification—for one is never either surprised
or mystified in a dream—the face of Gertrude
and Meta in one. Impossible to have said
which it most resembled, for it exactly resembled them both, and impressed me with
the idea that it *was* both, incomprehensibly but
none the less surely united in a single countenance. The strangeness and the horror of the
thing awoke me suddenly with real tears in
my cheeks—awoke me at the very moment
when Betsy, ignorant that I had come down
stairs, was ushering Mr. Wyke into the drawing

room, and explaining to him, with her usual volubility and communicativeness, the whole proceedings of the family during the day.

I was at first too drowsy and confused either to get up or to speak a word. I had a vague hope that Betsy would see me and take our visitor elsewhere before he could discover my presence; but that incorrigible individual, wholly engrossed with her own absurb chattering, did not see even glance towards the end of the room where my sofa was placed.

She would probably have hovered some minutes round the poor vicar, buzzing her gratuitous and unasked for information into his ear, had he not suddenly, and in a tone of quiet dignity that I thought sufficient to rebuke a dozen Betsys, said—" Thank you, I will trouble you now to let your mistress know that I am here."

Then, very unwillingly, and no doubt resenting this abrupt dismissal, Betsy vanished; and as Mr. Wyke was taking a chair she had set for him much nearer to the door than to me,

I managed to rise and to walk slowly (for I was giddy now as well as in pain) towards his end of the room.

Lost in thought, he did not immediately seem to hear the little rustling I made, but on my saying " good evening, Mr. Wyke," he started and looked up, very much as he might have done had a ghost appeared abruptly on the scene and accosted him.

I suppose my aspect was not very unlike that of a ghost to-night—moreover, the vicar had no idea that I was not at the Vivians' party. He had come, as he afterwards explained, to have a quiet half-hour with mamma, believing her to be without either of her daughters.

To my brief salutation, which I made as cheerfully and humanly as I could, under the circumstances, Mr. Wyke replied at first only by the start, and a look of almost terrified amazement. This passed, however, in a minute, and then his mind took in the truth of the case, and he got up before uttering a word and led me back to the sofa.

I submitted to him rather of necessity than
of free will, for of all things I detested playing the invalid, or being treated as one; but
my second nap had confused me, and done less
than the first towards mitigating the actual
pain I was enduring.

"Poor child! poor child!" he said, after
forcing my head back upon the pillow, which
he had shaken first into really delicious soft-
ness. "I have no need to ask what ails you.
One I nursed for years was subject to these
frightful headaches. You should not have
moved just now for anything or anybody. Did
you think I should exact ceremony from
you?"

"Thank you," was all I could say, so
touched I was by his extreme gentleness and
kindness, so grateful that this good, wise,
holy man, whom I looked up to as one looks
up to saints, should condescend to be tender
and even affectionate to me.

"Maggie's teacher," I said to myself again
and again; "don't be a fool, Ethel Beamish,

and forget so obvious a solution of the vicar's manner to you as this."

But he was sitting beside me, holding my burning hand in his own, occasionally laying his cool palm upon my hot temples ; now and then repeating, half absently, but always tenderly, " Poor child, poor child !" and do what I might, I could not help—venerating this friend as I did—I could not really help the upspringing in my heart of a sensation of joy and happiness, such as had never, even in dreams, come to me before.

By and bye, when I had assured him I was a little easier, he spoke to me in a low, soothing voice, of many things—of Maggie and his hopes and fears concerning her; of our school that we trusted to establish and make a living by; of our future prospects generally. Of Guy, in whom he told me he felt strongly interested; and then, impelled I know not by what impulse, unless it might be a yearning for a sympathy I was sure would be freely bestowed, I told Mr. Wyke all about my brother and Meta—all, at least, that did not involve the betrayal of Meta's own secret in reference to the vicar himself. I acknowledged frankly that I mistrusted my cousin, and that even could I believe that she would ever consent to marry Guy, I should deem her a most unfitting wife for him in all respects.

And having heard me patiently to the end of my story, Mr. Wyke said, in a tone of the very gentlest rebuke :—

" My child, I fear there is a tendency in your nature to run forward and meet the troubles that you imagine are advancing towards you. This is to live a double life of pain and anxiety, whereas our Heavenly Father has appointed to each individual but a single one. Guy is still a boy, and even if this attachment prove of the stubborn and unconquerable kind you say your mother and yourself think it is, several years must still elapse before he can dream of marrying. A few years, nay a few months, bring sometimes wondrous changes to us all. Let us therefore try to act as if we felt that wise and holy word which assures us that for weak mortal man 'sufficient unto the day is the evil thereof.'"

I thought it would be very easy to be wise if I had ever so kind and faithful and gentle a monitor beside me. He might have preached a dozen sermons to me this evening, and I should not have wearied of them or of him. Something—was it that strange tenderness of look and tone which had greeted me as I emerged from the land of dreams? was it a mysterious intuition suddenly revealing to me that, utterly unlike as we were, there was a hidden kinship between this man and me? or was it only that from physical weakness my heart to-night was weak and out of order too? I cannot tell, but something, I repeat, had certainly occurred to change (as far as my individual consciousness of the matter was concerned) the relations between Mr. Wyke and myself. It seemed to me that henceforth I must of necessity mingle in my great reverence for the pastor—whose dignity, whose age, whose acknowledged goodness, set him so immeasurably above me—the warm esteem, the grateful affection, the fond regard that we give to the best and dearest of our equals and friends. I need not betray to him or to any one that such feelings had been born in my heart. They were very innocent; they would do no mischief; they should rarely whisper their existence even to myself—but oh! were they not sweet?

Caressing them in this their earliest birth, I think I could have wept my life out for pure joy. I know I should have been content for time to have stood still, for there to have been no further change. I don't know whether my headache really left me, but I know I felt it no longer, not at least while he was with me; and he stayed till the summer twilight had given place to night, and the moon and the stars were looking into our quiet roo m. Mamma had joined us before this, but the vicar kept saying he was going, and petitioning against the introduction of candles, which he assured me would be bad for my head.

When at length he departed, I felt an extreme bodily weariness stealing over me, and I offered no opposition to mamma's suggestion that I should at once betake myself to bed.

CHAPTER III.

JANE'S OBSERVATIONS.

I SLEPT well that night, but wandered in no
more verdant forests, saw no more stagnant
lakes. If I dreamt at all, my dreams were
of the most commonplace kind, and when I
awoke in the morning I could have imagined
that the whole occurrences of the previous
evening, including those new, strange emotions I have attempted to describe, belonged
to the fantastic visions which had come to
me in the sleep I took by the open window,
with the summer air blowing in upon me,
and whispering, perhaps—as summer air will

whisper—the secrets of life's yet untasted bliss, the wondrous tale that, for all its birth in the Eden of our first parents, is never old.

The sun that shines garishly into our bed-rooms at about eight o'clock in the morning, warning us that it is time to get up and begin the prosaic duties of the day, has somehow a marvellous tendency to dispel the romantic and shadowy dreams which we may have indulged in by moonlight the night before. If mine did not quite make to themselves wings and fly away, at least they veiled their faces decently, and sat down in a meek, patient silence, waiting, and knowing that it might be for ever, till a voice from without should bid them rise.

But my pain and languor and weariness were all gone, and for this I was thankful beyond measure. In another hour life would be going on with me as usual, and what, at present, could be half so desirable as strength to fulfil the duties and accomplish the labours which circumstances, or, as Mr. Wyke would

doubtless have said, " Providence," had appointed for me?

To-morrow our first pupils were to arrive,
and we should assume by right the title of
schoolmistresses. Nothing very romantic or
heroic about this, was there? Far from it;
and yet I felt glad, and even happy, in
reflecting now upon the future that I saw
before me. It would be pleasant to hear
young, bright voices, continually around us,
pleasant to win perhaps the affection and
respect of those who might be committed to
our care, pleasant—well, Ethel Beamish, why
do you hesitate here, why do you shrink from
confessing, even to yourself, that above all
things in connection with this education work
it will be sweet to have the privilege of holding little Maggie Wyke to your heart
sometimes !

The sudden opening of my door very
cautiously and gently, and the intrusion of a
little white-capped head brought me instantly
down to the realms of common sense, and

made me blush to think how last night's dreams were still haunting me.

"Come in, Jane," I cried; "I am awake, and quite well again this morning."

"Oh, I am so glad," and Jane Norton, in dressing-gown and slippers, darted in, closing the door behind her, and soon making herself very comfortable on the bed beside me.

"Your sister is still asleep," she began, eagerly, "and I thought I would just pop in to see how you were, and to have a chat, if you happened to be awake. It was such a lovely party, you can't think, and everybody was so sorry you couldn't go. Miss Kauffman looked very pretty, and sang a great deal; and Mr. Hallam was there, and Alicia Clarkson of course. They didn't behave to each other as if they were engaged at all. I don't think Alicia could have been very well; she did not dance much, and I noticed, because I sat next to her, that she ate scarcely anything at supper, though it was really the most gorgeous supper I ever saw, with quantities of champagne—and such peaches and apricots, Miss Ethel! I thought how I should have liked to bring some home for you."

"Thank you, Jane, but I want to hear about Gertrude. Did she seem to enjoy herself in the least?"

At this question Jane became very excited and spasmodic—rocked herself to and fro on the bed, laughed, and then tried to look very sober, and finally said—

"May I tell you all I observed, Miss Ethel, and won't you be very angry, and say my imagination wants pruning, as you said the other day? Oh, I can't help noticing things; and it is such fun sometimes, and I do so love it. May I speak out."

"I shall be quite sick if you go on rocking the bed in that way, Jane. Speak out by all means, if it will keep that restless little body of yours in a state of quiescence. What have you observed now?"

"Well, only that a handsome young man, staying at Fell House, admires Miss Ger-

trude, excessively and is doing all he can to
make her admire him. They danced together
three times, and I know he asked her oftener
than that. He is the neatest and the daintiest
and the best dressed little man I ever saw ;
and I like his face, all except the lower part
of it, and he took your sister down to supper,
and talked to her in a half-whispering voice
all the time, and Miss Lizzie Vivian was
watching them, I know, as well as myself, for
I heard her say to her mamma later in the
evening, ' I do believe Walter's caught at
last,' and then she added something else that
I could not make out, but I saw Mrs. Vivian
frown slightly, and after that Lizzie said in a
coaxing voice, ' oh, do, do, mamma, dear,' and
her mother patted her on the cheek, and
looked as if she meant to give her what she
wanted. I wonder what it was, for we saw
all the presents she had had for her birthday,
and they were splendid. The young man
she called Walter, had given her a locket set
in emeralds. I suspect Miss Lizzie, though

she is only fifteen, thinks a good deal of that little dainty gentleman."

"But Jane, you have not yet answered my question relative to Gertrude. I wanted to know if she had seemed to enjoy herself."

"Frankly, then, I cannot answer you. I do not profess to understand Miss Beamish; she is so reserved, and quiet, and—proud, I was going to say, but that would make you angry, and I know she is very good and all that kind of thing, only her dignity sometimes repels people, and prevents them feeling at home with her. I don't think really she enjoyed the party much, though once or twice I did fancy she was seeming interested in that gentleman's conversation. I believe he is very clever. I heard others saying so—oh, and I danced a quadrille with him myself at the end of the evening. It was very kind of him to ask me, wasn't it?"

"That depends, Jane, on the degree of self-sacrifice involved in the condescension. Perhaps he had tired out all the other young ladies, and was glad to have recourse to you."

"No, I am sure it could not have been that. He was evidently a favourite with the whole party. And I am sure Miss Lizzie Vivian herself would willingly have danced every dance with him."

"Then we will set down his invitation to you, Jane, to the most exalted virtue. You have called him only Walter. I presume Kenyon was his other name?"

"Oh, yes; I had forgotten it. How romantic and like a novel it sounds; don't you think so?"

"Rather; but have you nothing more to tell me—nothing about yourself?"

"About myself! goodness, no, except that I enjoyed it all excessively. I danced nearly every time, and talked to a good many young ladies I had never seen before. I liked the music, too, of which there was plenty during the evening, particularly Miss Kauffman's singing, which everybody said was divine.

Mr. Hallam always stood by her and turned over the leaves."

"Oh, did he; and did my sister play at all?"

"Just one piece; she played it very beautifully, too, and that reminds me that soon after she had played, Mrs. Vivian called her aside, and had a long conversation with her alone. Of course I have no idea what it was about. Your sister was very thoughtful, and did not talk to me at all as we were driving home."

"Nor as you undressed and went to bed?"

"Oh, dear no, but then I am sure Miss Beamish looks upon me as quite a child, and incapable of entering into any rational conversation. Don't you think she does, now?"

"You *are* very childish, sometimes, Jane. Please don't begin rocking again, for I really cannot bear it this morning. And, hark! there is nine o'clock striking, so you had better run away and leave me to get up. Mamma will think we are all dead."

I was only partially dressed myself when Gertie, quite ready to go down, and looking as fresh and bright as if she had not lost a particle of her rest, claimed, in her turn, admittance into my room.

"Ethel, I have some good news for you— first, however, let me say how glad I am that you are better. Jane has been telling me that you are all right this morning. Your headache deprived you of a very pleasant party, but it was not of this I came to speak now. I got the promise last night of a new pupil—a boarder too. It is Mrs. Vivian's eldest daughter."

"Lizzie Vivian! you cannot mean it, Gertie."

"Indeed I do, and why not, Ethel? The child is tired of being at home; she has a great deal of spirit and does not like learning with her younger sisters, nor submitting to the same authority that is exercised over them. She has for a long time, it appears, teased her mother to let her go to school, but she only thought of coming to us last night. Mrs. Vivian feels as if this was a very pleasant compromise of the matter, as we are so near, and she can see Lizzie every week. Meta told me it would be a great relief to her to get rid of her eldest pupil, as she is difficult to keep in order, and exceedingly capricious in her fits of industry."

"Not altogether an encouraging prospect for us, then," I said, "though I suppose as schoolmistresses we must welcome anything and everything of the young lady genus. When will Lizzie come?"

"The beginning of next week—and as for the encouraging prospect, Ethel, don't for a moment imagine that Meta's report intimidated me. I will answer for keeping any number of high spirited young ladies in order, if only I am not interfered with by the parents. Are you coming down now?"

"Yes, in five minutes. Wait for me, Gertie dear, and tell me something about last night.

Did you dance much, and were there many nice people at the Vivians?"

"I danced a good deal—much more than I cared to do. For a wonder, there were more gentlemen than ladies, so all the girls got partners. Alicia and her lover were there of course. Meta was a great attraction, chiefly on account of her voice, though she looked remarkably well—in her evening dress, too. I did not notice that she flirted last night. Mr. Kenyon exerted himself to provide amusement for everybody. The Vivians seem very fond of him, and he is quite at home there."

From these disjointed pieces of information I could not gather much in reference to Gertie herself, but as we went down stairs together I said carelessly :—

"I suppose as Walter Kenyon was so busy amongst all the guests you had no opportunity of becoming better acquainted with him. I am a little curious about this young man, you see, because of Mr. Wyke's interest in him."

" Oh," replied my sister in the tone which I knew signified impatience at my questioning, " I believe I had him for a partner two or three times, and he happened to take me down to supper. He talks well, and is no doubt clever enough almost to justify the reputation he has acquired. But I am a bad judge of young men in general, Ethel. If you are desirous of learning more about him than can be gained from common report, you had better apply to Meta, who, living under the same roof, has doubtless abundance of opportunities for studying his character."

" It is fortunate that my anxiety on the subject will keep," I laughed in answer to this, "if Meta is the only person who can relieve it. We could scarcely see much less of our fair cousin if she were still in her happy fatherland, than we do at present."

" By the bye," said Gertrude, "that reminds me that Meta begged me to tell mamma she was coming to pay her a visit to-day."

CHAPTER IV.

OURSELVES AND OUR PUPILS.

META and Lizzie Vivian called together at
Lindenhurst on the afternoon of that day, but
Gertie and myself had gone down to the village to see the Downings, and take home their
niece, so we missed both our charming cousin
and her young companion, and my sister was
very much annoyed at having done so. For
my part I did not care at all. It had been pleasanter to me to sit and talk quietly with Miss
Dora, up and dressed to-day for the first time
since her attack, to hear how very, very kind
and attentive " dear Mr. Wyke" had been to

her, and how she was looking forward to his next visit when she should be able to receive and thank him personally for his neighbourly sympathy, and gifts, and constant calls of enquiry. Miss Downing was full of joy and gratitude at her sister's amendment, very pleased too to hear that Jane had amused herself at the Vivians, and a little elated, I think, in the prospect of entertaining Mr. Burns on the following evening—the one he had fixed for coming to drink tea at the cottage.

It was such a pity, kind Miss Harriet said, that Gertie and myself could not join their small circle, but the fact that our two first pupils were to arrive at Lindenhurst that evening was of course an all-sufficient reason for our declining the invitation.

" But you must positively allow me very soon to introduce you to him ; " continued the amiable spinster, with a little glow upon her still fair cheek. " Mr. Burns feels almost as much as I do the thirst for intellectual society, and you know, my dears, that at Gray-

bourne there is not a superabundance to offer
him."

"There is Mrs. Arnott," I said laughing—
"I have no doubt she would welcome gladly
the chance of a new victim; of course, Miss
Downing, you will send her an invitation for
to-morrow."

"Goodness forbid!" exclaimed Miss Harriet
with a look of real alarm. "I should be sorry
to expose any gentleman I respected to the
frivolities and coquetries of that very thoughtless little woman. I have nothing to say
against her, mind, and if I knew anything I
would keep it to myself—but her behaviour
to gentlemen is really so very——well," (and
Miss Harriet blushed more now than when she
had spoken of her wish of introducing us to
Mr. Burns) "well, it is really so entirely opposed to all my notions of propriety, that I
could never voluntarily become a witness to
it. You are not going to run away already,
my dears?"

But Gertrude was impatient, (she always

was when anything even remotely approaching to what she called "village gossip"
mingled with the conversation in which she
was taking a part), and so there was nothing
left for us but to say good bye and to express
a hope (this my sister undertook), that Jane
would be regular in her attendance at school,
conscientious in her studies at home, and a
pattern of industry and diligence generally.

"Isn't he soft, though?" whispered that
young lady to me, as after this speech of
Gertie's (to which both aunts had replied
eagerly "Oh, dear, I hope so,") she rose to
accompany us to the gate, hugging and kissing as she went the intelligent male object
she had referred to, and which perhaps it is
scarcely necessary to explain, was Blabberty
Cuetsums.

  o o o o o o

We began our work under really pleasant
and encouraging circumstances. The two
little girls who had been sent to us from a

distance, and over whom we were to have
entire control, proved quiet, docile, and not
particularly stupid children. They did exactly
what they were told to do, gave no trouble,
and learned about as well as girls of their
ages (one was nine, the other eleven), who
come to school for the first time, can reasonably be expected to learn.

Lizzie Vivian was a pupil of a different
stamp, and I cannot affirm that she gave no
trouble, because in point of fact she gave a
great deal both by her want of steady
industry, and by her undisciplined habits
generally; but then she was so clever, so
bright, so willing at times to make up for
past shortcomings, that it was impossible for
a teacher like my sister, whose whole heart
was in her work, and in the progress of her
pupils, not to feel a very strong interest in
her, not to accept the trouble gladly for the
sake of the ultimate reward. Except for an
occasional singing lesson, I had very little to
do with Lizzie in school hours. Gertrude

liked the girl, and took an extraordinary pleasure in teaching her; and Lizzie, though she was affectionate and caressing to us both, appeared to have conceived quite a romantic attachment towards my sister, and even out of the schoolroom followed her about, and hung round her as if she had no happiness elsewhere.

These three, living in the house, and not being wholly under our care, became naturally better known to us, and in some sense objects of greater interest than the other two of whom I am about to speak.

Jane Norton only came three times a week. She liked the study of languages, and got on well with them, so that Gertrude was not wholly dissatisfied with her as a pupil; but her music never progressed much, because she would not study it half enough at home; it was pleasanter, she acknowledged to me privately, teaching tricks to Blabberty Cuetsums or nursing the dear old cat; and then, as to drawing, why it was all very well to be

able to copy a picture in chalk or black lead,
and make it look like an engraving; but,
after all, that wasn't art, and Mr. Burns was
continually talking about art and artists, and
she should like to go to Rome and see the
wonders he told her about—the statues and
the pictures, and the buildings—and if she
couldn't be a real artist, she would rather
not attempt to draw or paint at all.

Of course Gertrude thought this childish
and silly in the extreme, and had Jane been
made subject to her control she would soon
have brought her to a more reasonable frame
of mind; but neither of Miss Norton's aunts
cared to lay a burden she would have winced
under, on the shoulders of the girl they had
adopted; therefore, Jane continued to do
pretty much as she liked, and to come to
Lindenhurst rather for her amusement than
for her mental profit.

And now there only remains my own
special little pupil, Margaret Wyke, to give a
report of.   The first day she came, led

shrinking and trembling into our big school-
room by her nurse, she made one spring on
discovering me, and nestling close in my arms
had cried, without a sound though, for about
ten minutes. After this, she had grown quite
calm and composed, had seated herself in a
little chair by my side, and during the few
hours she remained, had turned over and over
again, mechanically and abstractedly, the
leaves of a picture book I had prepared for
her.

The next day she had come into the room
bravely—had ventured to look furtively once
or twice at the other pupils, and having done
this, had continued cheerful till the evening.
The third day I began to teach her, and from
that time she was a source of the deepest interest and the most constant pleasure to me.
Quick, enquiring, thoughtful, and with a very
unchildlike earnestness in all she did, her
mind was just one of those in which it is not
only easy but delightful to sow the seeds of
knowledge and of truth. Of truth in its

highest sense, indeed, I soon discovered that Maggie knew more than myself—her father had taken care to teach her that—but he had left all the rest to me.

And so we got on together famously, and it was not long before Margaret began to enjoy the hours spent in the school-room nearly as much as she did the romp in the garden with which, whenever the weather permitted, I indulged her at least twice every day. Our other pupils had abundance of recreation also at proper times, but Maggie was the little one, the pet, the darling of the whole household, and but for me (who really loved her better than all the rest put together), I think she would have been spoiled instead of benefited by coming to school.

"I trust my little girl to your judgment, even more than to your affection for her," the vicar had once said to me; and I was determined that I would do my very best to merit the confidence reposed in me.

Except in the pulpit on Sundays, it hap-

pened that I did not see Margaret's father for
nearly three weeks after our school opened.
There was a good deal of sickness in the village about that time, and his few leisure
hours were claimed in many directions. It
was true he called twice at Lindenhurst
during the period of which I am speaking,
but I was from home on both occasions, and
so we had not met since the night of the
Vivians' party, when he had sat with me
in the twilight and made me forget how my
head was aching.

I wished sometimes, when I was tired
from the long day's teaching and the children
were amusing themselves in the garden, that
he would come in and spend an hour or so
with us. Teaching, to those who do not instinctively love it as my sister did, is rather
depressing work in the very hot summer days;
and somehow we had seemed especially deserted of late by the few neighbours, who
were wont, from time to time, to enliven us
by their visits. Mrs. Arnott was gone to the

seaside; the doctor and his wife had an infirm
relation staying at their house; the Miss
Downings were kept at home by the continued
weakness of the younger sister, and even
Alicia Clarkson had ceased altogether to show
her fair, serene face, at Lindenhurst. She
sent me a little note one day to tell me they
were all very busy preparing for a removal to
London, and that it was possible they would
not return to Beechwood till the middle of
the winter, when the wedding was expected
to take place. Alicia added that she hoped to
come and say good-bye to us before they
went, and then in a hurriedly written post-
script were these words, "Your cousin has
been a great deal at Beechwood lately. Mrs.
Hallam—" following this were two words
scratched carefully out, " delights so much in
her beautiful voice." The effaced words were,
I believe, "and Edmund." Why should
Alicia have blotted them out?

The third Sunday after Lizzie Vivian had
come to us she went home to spend the day,

and on returning in the evening she brought
us some unexpected news. The Fell House
party were on the wing also, going the next
week to Brighton or Worthing for a couple
of months, accompanied of course by their
governess, but leaving their guest, Mr. Kenyon, behind.

"What, alone in that large house?" asked
my sister, to whom Lizzie's information was
chiefly addressed. "Won't it be rather dull
for him?"

Miss Vivian laughed aloud. "I just fancy
Walter trying it," she said at length, when
her mirth had subsided, "though indeed,
to my thinking, what he is going to try is not
more than half a degree better. Only imagine, Miss Beamish, he has actually accepted
an invitation to stay with that prosy old
clergyman of yours at the vicarage!"

"Lizzie, I cannot permit you to speak of
Mr. Wyke or of any clergyman in that dis-
respectful manner," Gertrude said repro-
vingly, while I felt excessively inclined to

give pert Miss Lizzie a shaking. "Mr.
Wyke is a very good, a very clever, and I
have no doubt a very agreeable man; and in
my opinion Mr. Kenyon will be the gainer by
the companionship."

Lizzie bit her lips—she hated of all things
to be put down, even by Gertrude—but made
no further observations on the subject. Then,
to divert her thoughts from her temporary
humiliation, I asked her if she regretted now
having come to Lindenhurst, since but for
this she would have been of the party to
Brighton.

"I don't regret it in the least. I am very
glad to be here," she replied energetically,
and I wondered what peculiar attractions a
quiet home such as ours could have for a girl
like Lizzie Vivian.

The next day Meta came to bid us farewell, and after she had said a few hurried
words to Gertie and myself in the school-
room—we were too busy then to press her to
remain longer—she went down to mamma

and stayed talking with her for quite an hour.
That Guy and his hopes mingled a good deal
in their conversation I could not doubt, because I knew these would be uppermost in
my mother's mind, and because too she was
so very grave and thoughtful for all the remainder of that day; but neither to Gertie
nor myself did she make a single communication on the subject, and we had agreed,
since it was evident we had no influence, to
interfere no more in the matter.

It was on the evening of the same day that
Mr. Wyke came, instead of Maggie's nurse,
to take her home, and was persuaded by
mamma to stay and drink tea with us.

We made a large party that night round
the tea-table, and our vicar, who evidently
liked young people, was very cheerful and
agreeable. He was not seated near enough
to me for anything more than the interchange
of an occasional word or two, but I felt sure
that we should be drawn closer together

during the evening — was I not Maggie's governess?—and I was not disappointed.

My sister had promised to take Lizzie Vivian and the two little Munroes for a walk in the fields after tea, and knowing that in any case I intended remaining at home, she did not think it necessary to alter her plans on the vicar's account. When they were gone I asked Maggie if she would like to come out into the garden with me and play, while I read a little, or worked, under the trees on the lawn. I thought that mamma might enjoy a chat with Mr. Wyke alone, and that he could join me, if he cared to do so, later. But Maggie said she was rather tired and should prefer staying and looking at pictures in the drawing-room if I did not mind. Papa might go in the garden with me instead.

"And so he will," exclaimed papa, rising with a smile, before I could put in a word, "if Mrs. Beamish will kindly look after my little girl in our absence. Come, Miss Ethel,

I shall be a poor substitute for Maggie and your book, I know, but for to-night you must just make the best of me."

When we were on the lawn he asked me if I would walk or sit; was I tired, was I warm, had I a headache? and having obtained an emphatic " no " to all these questions, he decided himself that we would walk, as I had quite enough if not too much of sitting during the day.

" You don't enjoy this school keeping as thoroughly as your sister does, I believe," he added, half enquiringly, though I am sure he had settled the matter in his own mind before he spoke—" it wearies you a little sometimes —is it not so ?"

" Perhaps," I replied; " but how do you know ? how can you possibly tell anything at all about it ?"

" I judge from what I have seen of your character. Yours is a mind that requires greater variety of food and occupation than it can get from your present mode of life. The bodily inactivity, too, is repugnant to your natural instincts if I am not in error. Don't you often, when you take your seat in the schoolroom in the morning, knowing that you have to remain there for three or four hours, long ardently to be off over the hills and fields at the rate of half a mile a minute— anything rather than sit within those four blank walls teaching Lindley Murray and 'Pleasant Pages?'"

"He is not satisfied with what I am doing for Maggie—he considers me unfit to be her teacher," I said instantly to myself with a sinking heart, and something like a conscious- ness of injustice. Nevertheless I could not but reply frankly.

"If you are a magician and know people's inmost feelings, it would be useless denying them to you; but indeed, Mr. Wyke, I do not indulge either a spirit of discontent or a yearning for greater freedom that my work permits me to enjoy. I cannot help occasion- ally, when the sun is very bright, and the air very soft, and all things outside my blank walls very sweet and seductive, I cannot help at such times wishing to be free, and envying the idle birds who have nothing to do but to shout forth their gladness to their equally glad companions. Gertie is much better than I am. She never sighs to be beyond the dull room where her duties have to be performed."

"Well, I am glad, at least, that you are not blind to your own short-comings," he said in rather an amused tone, which I was disposed to resent, "this consciousness of error is the first step we are told towards amendment. Do you feel as if, with constant striving, you shall ever attain to the virtue of caring less for summer sunshine, and vagrant ramblings in woods and fields, than for Mrs. Trimmer and Magnall's Questions?"

I knew he was laughing at me now, and for the rare pleasure of seeing this grave friend of mine in a merry mood, I was willing to forgive him the impertinence. Still I could not help being anxious on the subject of Maggie; so after acknowledging that I feared I should never thoroughly love the work to which my life was probably to be devoted, I said, somewhat timidly:—

"I hope you are not very much disappointed in the progress Margaret has made. It is a short time yet, you must own, and she had been out of training for some months. I try to get her on—indeed I do."

Then he stopped abruptly, and took both my hands for a moment into his own, while an expression of deep gravity and earnestness overspread his features.

"My child, I can't thank you as I should wish to do. I can't take you down into my heart and let you read what is written there on this subject. You would be startled perhaps rather than gratified if you knew to what an extent I deem myself indebted to you for the kindness, the patience, the unwearying interest you have manifested in my little girl. Don't tell me that I cannot know anything at all about it. I have discovered it in her wondrous improvement, in her longing every day to get to school, in her strong attachment to yourself. These symptoms in a child like Maggie are not to be mistaken. And don't you understand that I appreciate all the more what you are doing for her from believing that teaching in general is distasteful to you? Well, you are nearly tired of listening to this long acknowledgment of obligation," (I am sure I was looking red and confused enough, but I was far from tired of listening to such pleasant words) " and so I will only say now, and this once for all— as Maggie's father I thank you, and as friend to friend I ask you to believe that notwithstanding the weight of obligation under which you have laid me, I do not feel it to be burdensome—I never could so feel it—but the reverse. Does this content you ?"

The foolish tears ran down my face (happily he was not looking into it) as I replied briefly, " Yes, but you strangely overrate my work and my merit in the case of Maggie; she learns so readily, and we understand each other so well, that I enjoy teaching her, indeed I do, Mr. Wyke. Now let us talk of something else."

"Presently," he said, as, taking my arm in his (we had stood still during the above dialogue), he moved slowly on with me again towards the wilderness end of our grounds, "but I want first to ask you one question which I am sure you will answer me truthfully. You make Maggie read a chapter in the Bible to you every day, and you talk with her about it. Do you do this because she happens to be the daughter of a clergyman, or because you feel that Bible knowledge should be the foundation of all other ?"

In the beginning of my acquaintance with Mr. Wyke I am sure I should have resented such a question as this, as savouring too much of priestly inquisition. I should have considered that he ought to be satisfied with the fact of my reading the scriptures with his

child, without enquiring into my motives for
so doing. But it was different with me now.
I never felt inclined for a moment to dispute
his right of questioning me on this or any
other subject—rather I esteemed it a privilege
and an honour to have excited so much of
interest in him as his probing my most secret
feelings seemed to imply.

But for all this, my answer to what he had
asked me was not ready immediately ; I must
be candid with myself as well as with him.
I must go down into the depths of my heart
and enquire there as to the origin of the
practice Mr. Wyke had alluded to, and concerning the proper motives for which he
evidently stood in doubt.

He gave me time for this self-communing,
appearing quite to understand why I was so
long silent, but listening with deep interest
and attention when at length my reply came.

" I believe I have made Maggie read the
Bible, not because you are a clergyman, but
because you are really good ; all clergymen

are not good, Mr. Wyke; I am afraid, though
I recognise as a fact that scripture knowledge
is the most important of any, I should not
have acted upon such a conviction had you
been otherwise than as you are.   If there
has been hypocrisy in what I have done, I
am very sorry; I did not intend to be a
hypocrite."

"Nor have you been," he said encouragingly,
and even warmly; "your motive, though not
the highest, was a kind and an unselfish one
—so kind towards me that I am emboldened
to ask a still greater favour of you—will you
hear it?"

"And grant it, too," I replied, elated by
his friendly approval; "I don't expect it will
involve a large amount of self-denial."

"I hope not," he said, gravely, "for it is
that you will read every morning to yourself
first, the chapters you intend going through
with Maggie, and that you will pray for God's
Holy Spirit to enlighten you as to the true
meaning of what you read."

Surely a very simple and proper request for a clergyman to make to a member of his flock, or even for a friend who knew and loved the truth of God himself, to make to another friend who was still ignorant and out of the way. And yet my jealousy was in arms again in a moment as Mr. Wyke thus gently spoke, and, as I thought, inwardly, " he is afraid I shall teach his child something wrong—he has no confidence even in my natural understanding of heavenly things."

I said, however :—

" I will certainly do this to please you, Mr. Wyke; but I am very careful in restricting my instructions to Maggie to those points which cannot be mis-stated or perverted. I have never meddled with doctrines, or questions of the least difficulty, I assure you."

There was—for I turned very cautiously to look at him—a placid, and I believe quite unconscious smile upon his face, as in answer to this uncalled-for self-defence of mine he said :—

"I have no fear of false teaching now, for Maggie. As regards head knowledge, at any rate, she has enough to preserve her from imbibing any erroneous notions even from teachers less enlightened than yourself. It was not, therefore, of Maggie's spiritual welfare that I was thinking when I made the request which you have promised to comply with."

"Thank you," was the utmost I could get out by way of answer, as touched, ashamed, penitent, and yet glad and joyous at heart, in the midst of all, I returned to the house to get my little pupil ready to go home with her father.

"Another time," he whispered to me, at parting, "I must find out what you mean when you call me 'really good.' I am so far from that, Miss Ethel, that if you could read my heart to-night, you yourself would be the first to admonish me, and to tell me I was one of those for whom King Solomon assures us 'the rod is made.'"

CHAPTER V.

THE GREEN BOOK.

PONDERING on these last words—marvelling greatly over them (for how, I asked myself, could I ever dream Mr. Wyke a fool in any sense?) I walked into Gertie's room which commanded a view far up the road leading to the village, and across the fields in front of our house. I wanted to see if my sister and her party were yet in sight; not, believe me, to watch the vicar and his little daughter going slowly in the homeward direction, though, as I could not help including them in the objects within reach of my vision, I did stand for a while gazing thoughtfully at their retreating figures, and picturing the quiet home life they led together—the father comforted for all want of companionship, for all mental loneliness, by the great and absorbing love he had for his little child.

Then, as there were no signs of my sister even in the distance, I turned from the window and sat down at the small table beside it, scattered over with copy books and pencil sketches, and other indications of schoolroom industry, which she had gathered here to examine and correct at her leisure.

But what is this book with the dark green cover, half hidden under some of Lizzie Vivian's faulty drawings, and with an ivory marker in it, as if it was in the course of being read? It does not look like a lesson book at all, and I have no remembrance of ever having noticed a volume bound in that peculiar green amongst Gertie's possessions before. Besides, she despises light literature

of every description, and rather boasts of never
having read half a dozen pages of poetry in
her life.

Well, what is it then—this mysterious
green stranger—appearing on the young
school-mistress's classic table, and evidently
by its position ashamed either of itself or of
her !

I take it up curiously and half afraid that I
am being guilty of an indiscretion—that I am
prying into something which is no concern of
mine.   On the title page I read " Poems—by
Alfred Tennyson."   On the fly leaf is written,
and this I read also in spite of the growing
mistiness of my understanding—" Walter
Kenyon, a friend's gift to one of the very few
who hear when poets sing."

" So, so," I said to myself, rubbing my eyes
hard, to be sure that I was wide awake, " this
gentleman with the gifted ears must assuredly
be possessed of a gifted tongue likewise, or
his pretty green volume would never be laying in the attitude of a familiar friend on

Gertrude Beamish's table. What next, I should be glad to know? and my looks went rapidly round the room in search of further tokens that might astonish and bewilder me. But there was nothing more to be seen. Very clearly it had not been intended for me to see even this.

Dear Gertie! was she afraid I should laugh at her, or blame her, or only fail to sympathize with her in her new and apparently secret studies? Was she really ashamed of having accepted the loan (for so I imagined his to be) of a book of poems, innocent poems, I was sure, from a young man whom she had met three or four times? Suddenly it occurred to me that perhaps, after all, Lizzie Vivian, who professed to be a great lover of poetry, might have borrowed this book from her friend, and brought it to school. I would find out from her some day, rather than ask Gertie any questions on the subject. If my sister did not choose to confide in me, I had a little pride of my own also, and would

not seek to know her secrets, were they small
or great.

I opened the book again at the place where
the ivory marker was laid. It was in the
middle of " The Lotus Eaters," which I read
from beginning to end, thinking it very
strange and very beautiful, but less interested
in my own impressions concerning it than in
speculating on the effect it would produce on
my sister's mind. There seemed such an almost ludicrous contrast between Gertrude's
own active, practical, ever busy life, the only
life that to her would bring the least enjoyment, and the picture of dreamy, contented,
delicious indolence given by this dreaming
poet in one of his most marvellous poems.
Would it be possible for her to enter into the
beauty of Tennyson's idea? The rare music of
the rhythm she could not fail indeed to appreciate; but would her mind see what the
mind of the writer must have been looking at
when he wrote of the " dark faces, pale," of
the " mild-eyed melancholy lotus eaters," and

of the golden dreams of the weary mariners,
who partook of the enchanted fruit!

If my sister's faculty of imagination had received the magic touch which could alone
throw wide its doors to admit the full
light of poetry, the question was—would she
ever again be satisfied with the dull, prosaic
duties, that had hitherto been all in all to her?
Would there not be a constant yearning and
pining for the indistinct, ineffable *something*
which life was not bestowing upon her!

But after these thoughts had crossed my
mind, I suddenly shut up the book and
laughed at my own folly. Gertrude was not
a weak girl of fifteen, to be beguiled into mazes
of romance and sentiment by reading a few
pages of a poet's fancies, however strange and
beautiful those fancies might be. She had
ever been a worker, not a dreamer; and constant, regular, not-to-be-evaded work has a
wonderful power in keeping the mind healthy,
and free from dangerous influences.

Why should she not read Tennyson then,

or any other work of imagination that might come in her way? Assuredly I could see no reason in the world against it; only the presence of this book on her table had taken me by surprise, and somehow I would rather it had belonged to anyone, supposing my sister to have received it direct from its owner, than to Walter Kenyon.

But, after all, it was no concern of mine, so I just put the volume back in the place from which I had taken it, and returning to the window, watched there till I saw Gertie and the children come in.

"We have had such a lovely walk," exclaimed Lizzie Vivian, beaming with animation and pleasure, as I joined the party down stairs. "We went as far as Briary Wood, Miss Ethel, just fancy! and have got lots of ferns and wild flowers. I never enjoyed a walk so much in my life!"

"That was a very long way for you to go so late in the evening," I said, addressing my sister, who had sat down on the nearest chair, and was looking rather pale and tired; "scarcely safe, either, I should think for ladies alone."

"We were not alone," replied Gertrude, speaking, I was sure, constrainedly; "Lizzie met her friend, Mr. Kenyon, and he discovered that he had a thousand things to say to her, so, as we could not stand, he walked on with us, and Fanny and Louisa begged to go to the wood. It was rather too far though, I think, and we are all tired."

As I went up with Gertie to her room, she continued, as if the matter required some extra apology:—

"I really did not know how to shake off Lizzie's friend when he had once joined us. He made himself so completely at home with the other girls immediately, and could tell them the names of every flower and fern they gathered. Lizzie was so pleased, too, which was natural enough, as he has been quite a member of her family lately; but this sort of thing won't do in a school—it must not happen again."

"When does he remove to the vicarage?" I asked.

"The end of this week. Did Mr. Wyke speak of it while he was here?"

"No; and I quite forgot to make any enquiries on the subject. Do you think now, Gertie, that Lizzie has anything to do with Mr. Kenyon's remaining in the neighbourhood?"

"Lizzie Vivian!" my sister exclaimed in evident amazement, "whatever can you mean? Why should she have anything to do with it? She is a child, Ethel."

"In years, but scarcely in character. You yourself speak of Walter Kenyon as her friend, and observe that she appears to take especial delight in his society."

"Which she may do very innocently, and with perfectly childlike feelings," said Ger-

trude, beginning to wax indignant. " Pray
don't invent a romance for any of my pupils,
Ethel, nor graft the sentimental follies of a
woman upon the simple, and, I hope, un-
spoiled nature of a child of fifteen."

With this she went into her own room and
closed the door, assuming that I had no intention of accompanying her beyond the
threshold.

" Proud heart!" I said to myself, "does it
feel already that the voice is gathering strength
and power which will one day call upon it to
surrender?   Does it throb impatiently and
entrench itself in armour of harder and colder
steel from the conviction that a siege is laid
against it which the heart with all its boasted
resources may yet be unable for ever to with-
stand !"

Poor Gertrude ! (for though she would have
disdained my pity I gave it instinctively) if,
by and bye, you shall be caught in the toils,
and wounded even mortally, you will bleed to

death before you will show your hurt; you
will hide it away, my darling, far more carefully than you hid the green volume I found
on your table this evening.

CHAPTER VI.

THE MISS DOWNINGS' TEA PARTY.

"Miss Ethel, we are going to have a tea-party, and I am to invite your sister and you, and Mrs. Beamish, first of all. Aunty Dora has received so much attention from every-body during her illness, that now she is better, Aunt Harriet thinks they ought to acknowledge the neighbours' kindness in some way. It will be great fun, I am sure. Blabberty Cuetsums is going to have a new cage, and a blue ribbon round his neck for the occasion. You *must* come, you know. Say you will, and then I will tell you more about it."

Such was Jane Norton's address to me as
she entered the schoolroom one sunny morning, about a fortnight after Mr. Wyke's visit.
And I replied :—

"I shall have great pleasure in coming
myself, Jane. I don't expect my sister will
leave the children, even if mamma remained
at home, but you can ask them both by-and-
bye."

"Well, I want you most of all" (in a
whisper), "because Mr. Burns will be there;
and we shall invite the vicar, and the doctor
and his wife, and Mrs. Arnott, who came
back yesterday; and, of course, the gentleman
stopping at the vicarage ; and Aunt Harriet
thought that if he came, you might bring
Miss Vivian with you. I don't know in the
least how we shall amuse them all, but I
daresay you and Miss Gertrude will play and
sing a little, and with Mr. Burns and the
vicar there is sure to be plenty of talking.
Then having tea will take up half the evening, so I suppose it will go off pretty well,

and the preparations for it will amuse my aunts beyond everything."

My sister, as I expected, excused herself from accepting the invitation, but said that Lizzie might go if she pleased; and as Lizzie did please—it was arranged that she should accompany me, mamma preferring to remain at home with her eldest daughter.

Jane did not appear at school on the day of the party; they would naturally be too busy at the cottage to spare any member of the small household. I had been entreated to come early, as it was so long since I had paid a visit to the amiable sisters, and they would like to have a chat with me before the "company" arrived. So as soon as the afternoon lessons were over, I went upstairs to get ready, leaving Maggie, who would not be fetched for another hour, in my sister's charge, and advising Lizzie not to make herself too smart for the quiet people she was going to meet.

When I went into the schoolroom again to

say good bye, I found Gertrude sitting there alone, busy over some exercise books, as usual, but looking, I thought, weary, and out of spirits."

"Dear," I said, on the impulse of the moment, "you need fresh air, and something to amuse you even more than I do. You work ten times harder. It is not yet too late for you to dress. Let me stay at home, and do you go to this tea-party."

"Not for the world, Ethel," replied my sister, while a flush that could have stood for nothing but determination rose to her face. " Don't you know how I hate tea parties, and how I punished myself going to the Vivians? My work here is quite sufficient amusement for me, and I shall either take the children for a walk, by and bye, or remain in the garden with them."

"I suppose you have sent them into the garden with Maggie now ?"

" Yes, the child seemed tired of sitting, and they will be sure to look after her till her nurse comes. I hope you and Lizzie will enjoy yourselves."

"Oh, no doubt we shall. Don't let Maggie stay out too long, Gertie, please; it is a good walk for her to the vicarage, and Mr. Wyke is so nervous about her if she looks in the least pale or tired. I suppose she can come to no harm with Fanny and Louisa."

"How absurd you are, Ethel! Anyone would think that child was made of wax to hear you talk. What harm could come to her in our own garden where she plays by herself every day?"

"Oh, I daresay it will be all right," I answered, a little ashamed of my fidgetiness; "but you see when she is alone she never goes off the lawn where I can watch her from the windows. They would not, however, think of putting her in the swing, would they?"

"Of course they would not. You know they are forbidden to get in it themselves unless we are with them. If you are anxious

I will send and have Maggie in at once, only
one likes to be alone sometimes."

Did I imagine it, or was there really a
mingling of bitterness and sadness in Gertrude's voice as she uttered the last sentence.
Anyhow it touched me, and bending down to
kiss her, I said :—

"Oh, let the child be. Nurse will be here
presently, and of course there is no danger.
I am sorry I said a word about it, but somehow the father's nervousness communicates
itself in part to me."

There was a peculiar smile on Gertie's face
as she lifted it then for a moment to mine;
and her tone was unwontedly affectionate as
she said :—

"A happy evening to you, Ethel, dear, for
you should be starting now; and here comes
Lizzie looking as bright and joyous as a May
queen."

We took the meadow road to the village,
and (I think I can answer for my companion
as well as for myself) enjoyed the walk

excessively. I was conscious of feeling very
happy that evening, not excited, not restless,
not anticipating any very novel enjoyment,
but just happy, contented, satisfied with my
life's cup of blessing, and only desiring that
it might be left to me for as long as I could
appreciate it as I did now.

Lizzie's mercurial nature prompted her to
talk, to express her pleasure in words, to communicate every passing impression, and to
claim sympathy---anybody's sympathy would
have done—with the half wild, girlish delight
she experienced in the anticipation of this
village tea party. But I was in no mood for
chattering or being chattered to, myself. I
answered her, civilly indeed, but not warmly.
I could not give up the sweetness of my own
thoughts for the sake of a madcap girl of fifteen, who, had my sister been present, would
not probably have remembered my existence.
But just as Lizzie—thoroughly spoiled child
as she was—disgusted with my taciturnity,
was beginning to pout and look offended, I

thought of Walter Kenyon's book of poems, and asked her if she had ever read Tennyson.

"To be sure I have, and know him nearly by heart," she replied, instantly. "Ask Walter to-night if he is there, and he will tell you all about it."

"I suppose Mr. Kenyon is a great admirer of Tennyson's works himself," I said, "and introduced them first to your notice. Does he lend you books now that you are at school, because you know my sister does not approve of romantic poetry for young ladies."

Lizzie laughed saucily, as she answered :—

"I have no books of poetry at school except manuscript ones full of my own compositions. I tell you I know Tennyson—all his best pieces at least—by heart, and have no need to refresh my memory by reading them again. What made you think I had borrowed books of Walter, Miss Ethel ?"

Now as I did not choose to tell this very knowing young lady that I had seen a volume belonging to her friend upon my sister's table,

I evaded her question in the best manner I could, and allowed her to gossip on in her own way—while I continued thinking—until we arrived at our destination.

We were the first comers, of course, but the gigantic preparations for this eventful entertainment were, happily, all completed, and the sisters sitting in festive attire, and with gracious smiles upon their pleasant faces, ready to welcome their visitors. Leaving Lizzie (who, as a stranger and a " Vivian," was to be received with a few extra honours) to the care of our zealous hostesses, I ran up-stairs to look for Jane Norton, and found her dressed also, and putting the last finishing touches, in the shape of vases of freshly gathered flowers, to the pretty bedroom where the ladies were to take off their " things."

" How charming you look !" she exclaimed, kissing me, and going into ecstasies over my very simple lilac muslin dress, to which I had added no ornament except a little bunch of white roses fastened with a pearl brooch in the bodice. "I am so sorry Miss Beamish would not come. My aunts are terribly disappointed, too, as they wanted to show her off to Mr. Burns. What do you think of Aunt Harriet?"

"I only saw her for a moment, Jane; but it struck me that she was looking wonderfully well and wonderfully young. I fancied it might be the effect of her light and very becoming toilet."

"Oh, no," said Jane, clapping her hands, and laughing delightedly, "the toilet has nothing whatever to do with it. Everybody observes the change, so it must be independent of dress. But, oh, Miss Ethel" (suddenly lowering her voice and speaking almost solemnly), "I sometimes think, though I would not say it to any one but yourself for the whole world, but I sometimes think—suppose he should not mean to propose after all!"

Jane's very unusual seriousness kept me from laughing outright at the oddity of this abrupt supposition, in which so much, both as to persons and events, was left to the imagination of her listener. I composed my countenance as well as I was able, and only said:—

" I conclude the ' he' stands for Mr. Burns, Jane, but you must really enlighten me as to what you mean by your ' after all.' "

Miss Norton raised the head of a drooping lily, and gave it the support of a young and vigorous moss rose; then she turned to me gravely, and replied:—

" There are some things, Miss Ethel, which we feel and see, but can never explain. I am not always at home when Mr. Burns comes; he may pay aunty more decided attentions when I am not present. I believe he must do so; because I know,—I am sure,—that she is living in a new world, and that he is the reason of it. If I could express myself better (but I am so stupid), you would understand me easily. I want to say that though it is not apparent to *me*, Aunt Harriet must have some good reason for thinking that Mr. Burns likes her, otherwise she would not have grown

so happy, or so young-looking in liking *him*.
Don't fancy, Miss Ethel, that I talk of this to
anybody else, or that any human being ever
hinted it to me—indeed, indeed it is not so;
but I cannot help having eyes, and at times
it appears to me so serious that I cannot help
either saying to myself—suppose poor Aunty
is mistaken after all."

"Suppose, for instance," I suggested,
scanning Jane's own face rather narrowly,
"that Aunty Dora should turn out to be the
attraction that brings this gentleman so often
to the college?"

"Oh, no," said Jane, quickly, "Aunty
Dora, if I am not mistaken, is beginning to
have hopes in another quarter, but I have no
right to speak of what I know so little at present. Will you come down?"

The guests were not long now in making
their appearance. First came the doctor and
his wife, then Mrs. Arnott, after her Mr.
Burns, and last of all, just as we were going
to sit down to tea, Mr. Wyke and Walter

Kenyon. For these two a place was made at
the large, sociable round table, between Miss
Dora and Lizzie Vivian, the latter getting Mr.
Kenyon next to her, and the vicar becoming
the neighbour of our youngest hostess. For
myself I was seated between Mr. Luke and
Mrs. Arnott, and I must confess that had I
chosen my own position it would not have
been exactly where it was.

Nevertheless the tea—the first important
part of a village gathering—went off admirably. The gentlemen talked, the ladies listened (with the exception of Mrs. Arnott, who
would talk too); there was a moderate dis-
play of wit, not unmingled with wisdom—for
had we not a vicar amongst us? a plentiful
sprinkling of merriment, and a universal desire to please and be pleased—elements which,
if properly amalgamated could scarcely fail to
produce an agreeable result.

I watched Mr. Burns with some curiosity,
and became pretty well convinced that what
I had all along suspected in reference to this

gentleman was the fact. Then I turned my attention to Miss Downing, and in so doing had to give Jane credit for a very clear reading of her aunt's state of mind. Unquestionably that excellent lady had gained admittance, lawfully or unlawfully, into fairy land, and was treading on brighter and sweeter flowers than any which even her youth had known I had no time now to reflect on what might be, when she was driven back into the wilderness where no flowers grew, nor any song of birds gladdened the still air. One dim vision of the heart awakened from a beautiful but cheating dream, flashed across my sight for a moment, and then I shut it out with a sick shuddering that seemed almost ominous, and fell to wondering what Jane Norton had meant when she spoke of her Aunt Dora having hopes in "another quarter," which must exclude from her any matrimonial ideas in connection with Mr. Burns.

She was looking very fair and pretty to-

night, talking, whenever the conversation
ceased to be general, in her low, quiet tones to
the vicar; and appearing, from a chance word
which floated over to me every now and then,
to be expressing a warm interest in the schools
and other benevolent institutions which he
was beginning to establish at Graybourne.
Could it be the vicar to whom Jane Norton
had referred as "another quarter?" why
indeed should it not be? Miss Dora was of a
very suitable age for him; she had a little
property of her own; she was a good, gentle,
interesting woman, and would, no doubt,
make an admirable stepmother to Maggie.
Everybody would commend such an union.
It would be altogether in the fitness of things.
How stupid of me not to have imagined such
a probability before—and yet, perhaps because it was a new idea, I could not immediately reconcile myself to it—nay, there was
an odd tightening of my heart strings which I
felt to be extremely absurd, under the circumstances, but which inclined me to rejoice

when Miss Downing gave the signal for rising, from the tea table, and we were all able to disperse about the room.

Fate, however, was against me just now, for as I stood leaning over a stand of flowers by one of the open windows, Mrs. Arnott (who could not succeed in drawing either of the gentlemen into a flirtation), came behind me with a whispered enquiry, as to how I liked the new vicaress we were so soon to have.

I turned calmly (for you see I was not quite taken by surprise), and asked her what she meant.

"As if you did not know!" she laughed, "who have never left Graybourne, whereas I only returned a few days ago. However, I believe you very learned ladies rarely condescend to listen to gossip, so unless you have heard it from either of the principals, it may be news to you that there is a marriage in contemplation between our saintly vicar and one of the fair sisters by whom we are being entertained to-night. The whole village is talking of it; and have you not observed how they keep together this evening? How she managed to win him I cannot even conjecture, for between ourselves I have never been able to get even a civil word from him, and that the offer came from him no earthly power should ever make me believe. It will be fine fun, though—a wedding in the village—and the other sister, as you can see, is angling with all her might to catch that stiff old Burns. She won't manage it, though, for literary men, as a rule, hate your strong-minded females. By the bye, you have met Mr. Kenyon, I understand, before this evening. Do tell me what you think of him? I am determined to make friends with him by and bye, in spite of that precocious little Vivian, who is trying to keep him entirely to herself. She has just got him into a corner with a chess table between them, as if a baby of her age could play at chess! It is rather lucky, though, your having her for a pupil

—the connection is so good—I hear that you and your sister teach admirably, and are, in short, model school-mistresses. I have a great mind to come to school myself by way of a change. Gracious! how those men are talking at the other end of the room. One can scarcely hear one's own voice. Why don't they try to make themselves agreeable to the ladies?"

I did not attempt to interrupt the loquacious widow during the whole of her lengthy and rambling speech. But when, from mere exhaustion, she paused and sat down close to where I was standing, I said (not to appear quite uninterested in her communications) :—

"Have you any good authority for believing that the lady you first spoke of is engaged to be married?"

"My dear creature," she replied, lightly, "what a question to put to me, as if I ever troubled myself about authorities or any such bewildering things. I only know that the discriminating public of Graybourne have thus setttled the matter, and that there are heaps of circumstantial evidence to corroborate it ; for instance, the vicarage has been freshly papered (with very light paper too) throughout—the drawing-room has had, or is having, a new carpet and curtains. Maggie, as you are aware, goes to school, and—let me see—my Susan has heard, through the Miss Downings' Phoebe, that ever since Miss Dora's illness the vicar has been to see her nearly every day, and stayed for a couple of hours sometimes at a stretch. Then, too, there have been mysterious parcels arriving by the carrier from London addressed to Miss Dora, and having every appearance of coming from a ready-made linen warehouse—in short the whole thing is as clear as noonday ; but hush —Miss Harriet approaches us, and I have already, on your behalf, wasted far more eloquence than I am in the habit of expending at an evening party on any one of my own sex. I small go now and spoil Miss Lizzie Vivian's chess playing. The idea of a monkey like that monopolizing the only agreeable and good-looking man in the room !"

" My dear Ethel, we want you very much to play some little thing," said Miss Downing, as the flighty widow made her escape. " Jane has been attempting to set the example, but she is nervous to-night, and does not do herself justice. Our friend Mr. Burns is excessively fond of music. Will you come to the piano ?"

I could not refuse her, although I had never felt less inclined to exhibit my really small talent in public. I knew, however, that nobody would listen to me after the first five minutes. Glancing round the room I saw Lizzie and Walter still at their chess-table, and Mrs. Arnott bending, with her most captivating smiles, over them. I saw Jane Norton playing show-woman in her own eager and enthusiastic manner to Blabberty Cuetsums, for the benefit of Mr. Burns, who was listening to her as gravely and attentively

as if she were dilating on some rare pheno-
menon of nature, instead of on an ordinary
grey dormouse. I saw a group of animated
talkers composed of the doctor and his wife,
and the vicar and Miss Dora, with some books
of choice engravings on the table before them,
and I assured myself that my poor playing
would receive no notice, excite no criticism
whatever.

So I selected a piece which was a favourite
of my own—a nocturne that always took me
into dreamland and soothed me when my
spirits were ruffled or depressed. It was a
good instrument that I had to play on, and
I believe I played my best, not from taking
unusual pains, but because I felt the melody,
and suspected that I was ravishing my own
ears alone.

When it was finished, and before I could
leave my seat, there came a little murmur of
applause and thanks from several voices. I
did not detect the vicar's amongst them, and
I was just wondering whether he cared for

music (I knew Miss Dora did not play) when turning suddenly round I was startled to find him standing close behind me.

" I never heard you play till to-night," he said, " and I have enjoyed it. Come and let me show you some of these views of Palestine that we have all been looking at. There is that little table by the window where we can examine them nicely. Are you quite well ?"

" Yes ; thank you."

I felt as if the growing heat of the room was suffocating me, and could only get out that brief answer disjointedly.

" Because," he said kindly, " you have less colour than usual, and I was afraid you might be threatened with a headache."

" No—oh no—only the room is very warm."

" That is why I propose taking you by the open window."

So we went, and he brought the book of engravings and laid it between us on the small table ; and then he gave me an easy

chair and took another beside me; and when
this was done he asked me again if I was
sure I was quite well; and the engravings
remained untouched because he said my
voice and look contradicted the assertion I
repeated of having nothing at all the matter
with me.   But by degrees as we talked
together—or rather as he talked, and I
listened—my spirits rallied, and the heat of
the room ceased to oppress me.   Then I
exerted myself to talk too, and wishing to
choose a subject that must be interesting to
him, I spoke of Maggie.

"By-the-bye," he said, interrupting me
almost at the first mention of his child's
name, "I had forgotton to tell you that nurse
was detained to-night when she ought to have
started for Lindenhurst, by the unexpected
arrival of a relation.   I desired her not to be
above an hour after her usual time, and even
this I felt was more than I should have con-
ceded, being unable, on account of our meeting here, to go for Maggie myself.   I hope,

however, your sister and mother will not
have found her greatly in the way.   I would
have sent my housemaid, only she is given to
gossiping and lingering on the road, and I do
not like to trust Maggie with her."

It seemed very absurd that, as Mr. Wyke
spoke, a vague feeling of uneasiness, resem-
bling that which had caused Gertrude to
laugh at me earlier in the evening, should
have insinuated itself into my mind, and
made me wish beyond all things for the
knowledge that Maggie was safe at home.
Certainly if nurse had gone for her an hour
after her usual time, it must be all right, or
we should have heard ere this. As I pondered
and calculated, forgetting to reply in any
way to the vicar's apology, he looked at me
in some astonishment and said :—

"I am afraid I have done wrong. Perhaps
your mother and sister wished to go out.
Perhaps—"

A very loud and violent ringing at the
garden gate arrested his words, and startled

us both. I felt my heart begin to beat audibly.
I was frightfully nervous to-night, and this
nervousness made me connect the impetuous
pulling of the bell at that late hour with the
subject occupying my thoughts.   The curtain
had just been drawn before the window, and
the lamps brought in.   It was not my place
to rush out into the passage of the Miss
Downings' house to ascertain who their
impatient visitor might be ; and yet I did it
on the irresistible impulse of the moment,
arriving just in time to catch the first glimpse
of Betsy's scared and heated face, as the
servant of the cottage opened the front door,
and made way for me to thrust myself
before her into the porch.

CHAPTER VII.

A BROKEN ARM.

" Oh, Miss, to think of its being you as I was to see first! but it's the doctor we wants, and not to lose a minute; we can't bring her to no how, though your ma's being trying this half-hour, and says she's only fainted from the pain and the fright; and Miss Fanny and Miss Louisa they're crying their hearts out, and Miss Gertrude not taking no notice of them, she's so angry, and looking as white herself as if she was a going to faint too; and then I says to Missis 'let me run down quick and fetch Mr. Luke and Miss Ethel from the

party,' and Miss Gertrude wrings her hands
and says to herself, 'my sister will never
forgive me,' and Missis after thinking a bit
says, 'you had better go, Betsy, but mind the
vicar's there too, and it would be best if we
could get the doctor here before he knows
what has happened. God help us,' she says,
'if any serious harm comes to the child, for it
would be a'most the death of him,' and then
Miss Ethel I set off, and have run every step
of the way."

I had literally not strength to interrupt the
panting and gasping girl till all the above had
been spoken. I was clinging to the frame-
work of the porch to support myself while I
listened to her, for my head swam round,
and my knees trembled as if some terrible
physical malady had abruptly seized me.
But, at the first pause Betsy made, a little
presence of mind returned to me, just
sufficient to enable me to ask if Maggie had
been thrown from the swing, and, on
receiving an affirmative answer, to devise a

scheme for getting Mr. Luke away without arousing the suspicions of the vicar.

Miss Downing's Phœbe still stood at the front door, listening with open eyes and mouth to what was passing between Betsy and myself. I turned to her, and in a low voice, which trembled almost too much to be intelligible, gave her my orders. She was to go at once to the drawing-room and say that Mr. Luke was required for a sick child in the village, that he must please to come directly, as it was an urgent case, and then she was to contrive to let Miss Downing know privately that I wanted to speak to her outside, and after that to bring me my bonnet and shawl from the bed-room.

I had scarcely finished giving these directions when a tall, dark figure, brushed swiftly past me, emerging apparently from a corner of the ill-lighted passage behind Phœbe, whose Amazonian figure was quite capable of concealing two moderately sized individuals. In a moment I guessed the truth, and even cried out I believe, aimlessly and fruitlessly in my sincere distress.

Mr. Wyke had somehow comprehended my first suspicion concerning the loud ringing of the bell, had followed me, unobserved, from the drawing-room, and had heard all that had been said. Why he did not rush off at the first sound of Maggie's name, and why he went now without a word or a sign to me, I could not imagine; perhaps his mind, like my own, had received an almost paralyzing shock, and he was conscious but of the uncontrollable impulse to get at once to his child. I turned very sick and faint in reflecting on what his feelings would be when he saw his Maggie, his darling, the one treasure of his life, lying pale and senseless on the bed, with mamma and Gertie, weeping, perhaps helplessly, beside her. But this was the moment for action, not for brooding thoughts. Mr. Luke might be told the whole truth fearlessly now, and luckily he was near enough to his surgery to fetch anything he might require

in the way of restoratives (I dared not yet
even to myself admit the possibility of broken
limbs), before starting for Lindenhurst.

In the few minutes from the time Mr.
Wyke had vanished down the road, the
doctor was in possession of the whole facts of
the case as I was able to gather them from
Betsy's account. In a few minutes more the
latter was despatched with a written order
to the surgery, and Mr. Luke and myself
were on our road to Lindenhurst.

" I will see to the sending home of Miss
Vivian," Miss Downing had kindly said to me,
as she helped me to tie on my bonnet ; " and
do try, my dear, to keep up your own strength
and courage for the poor father's sake. He
will, of course, stay at your house with his
child to-night. Jane shall come down to
enquire after you all in the morning."

I remember a passing wonder as to how
this calamity would affect Miss Dora in her
still ailing and nervous state, and then she
went, curiously enough, out of my mind alto-

gether as connected in any way, present or future, with the friend whose sorrow I can truly say was already my sorrow.

I don't know how long it took Mr. Luke and myself to get Lindenhurst. It seemed an age, and yet we must have walked at a very rapid pace to judge by the utterly exhausted state in which I arrived at home. The little man had not distressed me much by talking to me on the way. Once or twice he had said—"This is a bad job, Miss Ethel, a very bad job ; the child hasn't the constitution of a feather ; " but as I did not even attempt to answer him, he never went beyond these sudden outbreaks, and I was more grateful to him for his forbearance than he ever knew.

Gertrude was standing at the gate as he came up, watching eagerly for Mr. Luke, and shivering, though it was such a warm night, from the nervousness and dread which had taken entire possession of her. She seized my hand as I approached her, and appeared incapable for the first minute or two of uttering a word.

"Where shall I find the little girl?" said the practical doctor, rightly judging that there was more important work for him in-doors than out. "I don't want either of you with me yet; the fewer there are in the room with her the better, and I suppose the father has arrived."

"Yes," Gertrude replied now, still holding me tightly, "and they are in mamma's bed-room, Mr. Luke—you know the way to it."

He was off in a moment, and then poor Gertie let go my hand suddenly, and burst into tears.

"Ethel, it was all my fault. I began reading after you left, and forgot to have the children in. Something had delayed our tea far beyond the usual hour, and it seems Maggie grew tired, her nurse not coming for her, and Fanny and Louisa thought there would be no harm in giving her a little swing just to amuse her till I should call them

indoors.   The child must have become either
giddy or frightened as soon as she was high
in the air, for they know nothing but that
her hands abruptly released the ropes, and
she herself was thrown, violently, of course,
as they acknowledge to having swung her
rapidly, on to the lawn.   It was a mercy
that the grass was long and thick; had she
fallen on hard ground she might have been
killed on the spot; but it is bad enough as it
is; I shall never forget Mr. Wyke's look as
he stalked in, pale, and stern, and speechless,
ten minutes ago, and gazed down at the
child."

In giving me this hurried recital, my
sister's agitation had in some degree subsided ;
she had evidently dreaded the first interview
with me, and was relieved to have it over.
I would have been more tender with her had
her excitement and distress continued unaba-
ted, but I was glad, too, that she had grown
calm, because I had fifty questions to ask her
before I went into the house.

"Gertie," I said, "it is not for me to blame you even were it clear that you might have prevented this accident. Tell me first if Maggie has been recovered from her fainting fit; I shall have hope for her when once that is done."

"Oh, yes; I thought you knew," she answered eagerly. "Her nurse arrived just after Betsy had started for you and Mr. Luke. The woman was nearly beside herself for a few minutes, when she saw the consequences of her own neglect; but mamma desired her not to waste any more time, but to see what she could do towards restoring the child, all our efforts having failed. We had been afraid, knowing how delicate Maggie is, to throw cold water over her, but nurse immediately dashed a great jug full in her face, and this revived her. Then, with much difficulty, for she is evidently hurt somewhere, we got her clothes off, and had just laid her, nearly fainting again, in mamma's bed, when the vicar arrived. I did not stay two minutes in

the room after his entrance—he frightened
me, Ethel—but came out here to watch for
Mr. Luke. Don't go in yet—you can do no
good; and see, there is somebody coming
from the house; we shall hear, now, how she
is, and what the doctor says."

It turned out to be Maggie's nurse, and the
poor old woman was crying bitterly. She
told us she was going, as quick as she could
walk, to Mr. Luke's surgery, for a number of
things he wanted, that Maggie's right arm
was broken, and must be set to-night, that
the vicar would stay at Lindenhurst, and
finally that the poor little girl had taken a
spoonful of wine, and had just asked for me.

"Then I must go to her, Gertie," I said,
as nurse hastened away, and left us again
alone. "Don't stay out here, dear, any
longer. I will come frequently to your room
and tell you how we are getting on. Poor,
sweet little Maggie!"

"This is dreadful, though," whispered my
sister, shivering as she had been doing when

I first met her at the gate, "and you are as
white and cold as a ghost yourself, Ethel.
You will not attempt to be present while the
arm is set; pray don't—it would be too much
for you, and as Mr. Wyke is here—"

"Yes, as he is here," I replied almost
indignantly, "he shall not be without the
very little support and comfort I can give
him by my presence. What do my sufferings
matter ? it is theirs we have to think of. I
would have lost both my own arms to have
saved the father and child from this."

I spoke more warmly than I ought to have
done, because I could not help thinking
Gertie somewhat selfish in the matter. I
believe now it was nothing of the kind, that
she was only very, very frightened, and full
of remorse for what she considered her own
part in the calamity—but at the time I was
much too excited for the exercise of any rational judgment, and so I wronged her
cruelly, this dear, dear sister, whose evil

days were even then coming up out of the misty future to meet and overshadow her.

*   *   *   *   *

He did not speak a word to me. He did not even appear to know when I entered the room, although I walked up straight to the bed—composing my countenance as well as I was able—and took the tiny, white, *left* hand that Maggie, with the faintest of smiles upon her pale lip, instantly stretched out to me. He, the father, was sitting on the side nearest to the broken arm, which at present was carefully covered by the bed-clothes, and his hand was straying, I think unconsciously, amongst the tumbled golden curls of his Maggie's hair, while his eyes, in their rapt, silent, earnest gaze, expressed far more elo- quently than any words or even any tears could have done, the fathomless depths of love and pity that were in his heart for her.

Poor little motherless girl! In this her

hour of trial and heavy suffering, she must not feel that she has lost the parent who would best have soothed and pitied, and helped and comforted her.

Mamma and Mr. Luke had both looked up and said a word to me as I came in. The former sat at the bottom of the bed preparing bandages, and with a deeply distressed look upon her kind face ; the latter stood on the side to which I had gone, feeling from time to time the pulse of his little patient, and administering some drops from a bottle he held in his hand. Betsy had returned from her errand to the surgery before I came into the room, and we were now only waiting for nurse, who was to bring what the surgeon needed for setting the broken limb.

It seemed a very long time that she was away, but then any waiting in a sick room for remedies which are to give relief to the sick person always does seem interminable, and when a child is the sufferer—a little,

gentle, patient, delicate child, like Maggie—
such waiting and watching must ever be
especially trying to the lookers on.

It would have been an immense relief to
me if Mr. Wyke had spoken, during all this
time, a single word—if he had even blamed
me, accused me, reviled me as the indirect
cause of his darling's misfortune. I felt
keenly and bitterly enough myself that I had
done wrong in not yielding to the impulse
which, before I left home, had urged me to
see Maggie safe in the house by my mother's
or Gertie's side. But Mr. Wyke · did not
know of my misgivings—he could only
blame me for having gone to the tea-party
while my little charge was still at Lindenhurst, and in spite of his exceeding love for
her I thought he was too just a man to do
that. Why would he, then, not speak to me,
not look at me? Had I suddenly become
hateful to him, or was he really unconscious
of my presence, though Maggie often looked

from him to me and smiled, poor darling! with equal sweetness upon us both, when she could smile at all.

But nurse came at last, and then the dreary stillness of the room was broken. Mr. Luke took possession of what was brought him, and with a brisk, though courteous, "by your leave, vicar," displaced the father from the position he had hitherto occupied, and told him he might go for a bit out of the room.

"Not unless you absolutely order it," said Mr. Wyke, firmly, though I saw, and trembled in seeing, that he had suddenly become pale as death. "I can surely bear what this little one will not shrink from, with me by her side, eh, my Maggie; shall not papa stay with you?"

"Yes," whispered Maggie, faintly, for in truth the poor little heart sank at the anticipation of what was going to be done to her; "and you, too," directing a pleading glance towards me, "you will not go away."

"Not for the world, darling," I said, looking at her through blinding tears that would come now, do what I might to stop them. "I will not move from your side for as long as you care to have me."

Then the father, who had been speaking to mamma as she left the room (her nerves were not strong enough for what was coming), moved to where I stood, and laid his hand kindly on my shoulder.

"My child, I did not intend that you should be exposed to this. It never struck me that Maggie would ask it of you. Can you bear it, do you think, so pale and weary as you look? I would much, much rather send you from the room."

"And I would much rather remain in it," I said, speaking low as he had done, and forcing back my tears that he might not observe them. "If you and Maggie can endure it, I should be a coward, indeed, to seek an escape; but, Mr. Wyke," I added, by a sudden impulse as I felt the hand on my

shoulder trembling, " can you bear it; are
you strong enough ; is it right that you
should try ?"

"Quite right," he said, almost smiling at
my earnestness, I suppose; "and with you to
help me with your brave spirit—you shall
see how brave I can be."

Oh! if he had known how unlike a brave
spirit mine felt at that moment! but perhaps
he did, and only so spoke to excite in me the
courage he saw was miserably lacking.

There came a little piteous " oh !" from
poor Maggie, as Mr. Luke's first touch fell
upon the broken arm, and at this sound I ran
to her and held her left hand tenderly and
soothingly in my own, while the father,
covering his face with his hands, sat down
just behind me, and neither spoke nor stirred.
I could not even hear him breathe, though I
could guess that his every breath was a sup-
plicating prayer, till it was all over.

" Beautifully, beautifully borne, my little
lass, and not badly set," exclaimed the well

pleased doctor, running for the wine and handing a good glassful this time to his exhausted patient. "Now, vicar, you may come and give the young lady a kiss, and then I shall turn you out of the room for the night. Miss Ethel is to be my sole coadjutor for the present, and I think you may trust us both for doing our duty to Miss Maggie here, till you see her again in the morning."

The father made not the slightest resistance to these orders now. His countenance was still strongly agitated, but it had lost the perplexed and brooding look that it had worn when I first saw him in the sick room.

"You think it will be all right with her?" he whispered to Mr. Luke, after he had bent down to kiss his darling's white cheek, and to receive her almost inaudible good night; "you have no fears now?"

"Few, if any," said kind Mr. Luke, shaking him heartily by the hand, "she must be taken care of, you know, and it may be (with a smiling glance at me), that her governess may have to become her nurse for a while, since they seem so well to understand each other; but that will be no great matter, I suppose. Now take that pale young lady down to get some supper, and send up madam nurse to receive my instructions for the night."

He would not listen to my assurances that I wanted no supper, that I would prefer staying with Maggie, at least till nurse came to take my place. "You must come to please me, if not yourself," he said, with his kindest look and smile; and so I went with him to the dining-room where mamma and Gertrude were anxiously waiting for news from up-stairs, and because the vicar poured it out, and insisted on my drinking it, I took a glass of wine, and ate a crust of bread, which did me good, and checked the strong hysterical symptoms of which I had been so painfully conscious for the last hour.

Then mamma went away to prepare a room for Mr. Wyke, Gertie to receive Lizzie

Vivian, who had been brought home by her
friend Mr. Kenyon; and I, after an almost
tender "good night," and a sweet "God
bless you !" from Maggie's father, went
again to the little sufferer's bedside, and
remained there with Mr. Luke and old nurse,
till towards morning the weary child slept
herself, and they sent me off, peremptorily,
to get what rest I could, during the few hours
dedicated to repose that were still left to us.

CHAPTER VIII.

NOT ALTOGETHER PLEASANT.

MR. LUKE would not have stayed at Lindenhurst all through the night if he had not still
feared that things might go wrong with
Maggie even now. Her constitution was so
extremely fragile that had any amount of
fever succeeded the setting of her arm, there
would have been no answering for the result.
This he told me in the morning, when a good
sound sleep had put danger for the child
nearly out of the question, and when the
vicar, after one look at her, one kiss, one
whispered word of praise for all the courage

and patience she had manifested, had gone
home to his vicarage, and to the guest waiting for him there.

"I had only a single fear in leaving
Maggie in your charge," he had said to me
as, at his own request, I walked with him, in
the fresh, lovely morning, as far as our
garden gate; "and that is that you will
wholly forget yourself and tax your own
strength needlessly.   I will not ask you to
promise anything, because I should have no
faith in the performance of your promises,
but I promise you—mind, this is not a threat
only—I promise you to have Maggie brought
home, at any risk, the moment I find you
are doing more than you ought to do for
her."

"Very well," was my cheerful reply, "I
am content to have it so; you do not frighten
me in the least.   Good morning, Mr. Wyke."

"Good morning, Miss Ethel; I shall be
here early in the evening."

Soon after breakfast came Jane Norton

with the kindest messages from the cottage,
and the most anxious desire to be made use
of herself in any way that we could suggest
to her.   The vicar had called, she said, in
passing, and told them that Maggie was
doing well, and they were all so glad and
thankful.   Aunt Dora had scarcely closed her
eyes for the night, picturing all sorts of
horrors, and fancying every gust of wind was
Maggie screaming.   " And then," continued
Jane, " Mr. Wyke told her how good and
brave you had been throughout, and how
grateful he was to you.   Both my aunts
think he likes you much better than your
sister.   I don't see anything strange in this,
but then the vicar does not know you so well
as I do."

And Jane, whose heart I had managed
somehow to win, put her arm round my neck
and kissed me affectionately before she went
away to the performance of a little task I had
set her.

I spent the greater part of that day reading

aloud to Maggie, who was too weak to read to herself, and could not bear me to be long absent from her. Gertrude would not hear of my assisting her in the school-room; she was in one of her cold, reserved, almost stern moods, and evidently preferred being without me.

The two culprits of the night before, though they had received no actual punishment, trembled each time they encountered my sister's look of grave displeasure, and even Lizzie Vivian, favourite though she was, must have met with less indulgence than usual to judge by the subdued, I had almost said sulky expression, that was clouding the brightness of her pretty face when we met at dinner.

For myself I was beginning now to feel a little the effects of the sleepless night and the hours of anxiety I had undergone. My head ached, and I was out of spirits; I did not want my dinner, and mamma's kindly meant importunity on the subject worried me unreasonably, though I tried not to appear bad tempered, and was vexed that I succeeded so ill.

"Don't be cross, my dear Ethel," said Gertrude, as for a second or third time I refused, perhaps somewhat petulantly, what she had been urging upon me. "It is for your own sake we want you to eat, for if you are going to be chief nurse to that child all the time she remains ill, I am sure you will need to keep up your strength."

I said nothing till the pupils had left the table for their half-hour's recreation in the garden. Then some of the thoughts and feelings which all the morning had been pursuing me, found vent in the assurance I gave my mother and sister that there was no chance of my continuing Maggie's head nurse, inasmuch as her future step-mother would doubtless claim her right to take my place, and to do everything for the child that servants could not do.

I knew that the gossip occupying the village just now must soon come to their ears, and I had a fancy that I should like better telling it to them than having them tell it to me.

So on mamma's questioning me with surprised looks, as to what I could possibly mean, I repeated word for word what I had heard from Mrs. Arnott, not omitting the fact, which had appeared rather significant to me, that Mr. Wyke had gone considerably out of his way in the morning to call at the cottage, and give the sisters the earliest intelligence concerning Maggie.

"I don't believe a single syllable of it," said Gertrude, decisively, while I could almost have believed that her eyes grew softer and tenderer as she looked at me; "and I think you are very weak, Ethel, in listening to anything from that marvellously silly woman. Is it likely, now, that the vicar, if he wanted to marry again, would choose a perpetual invalid—a poor, nervous, useless creature—however amiable—such as Miss Dora?"

"I am not so sure of that," replied mamma,
reflectively. "It is a curious fact that clergymen do manage almost invariably to get delicate wives, and in every other respect than
her health Miss Dora would be suitable
enough for the vicar. Mrs. Arnott is certainly no authority, but I had heard myself
that Mr. Wyke had lately been a good deal
at the cottage."

"And what of that!" exclaimed Gertie,
getting quite hot and indignant, "has not the
younger sister been ill, and is it not a clergyman's duty to visit the sick—oh! how des-
picable, how paltry, how hateful all this senseless gossip appears to me. I have really not
patience to stay and listen to it."

And so she went to her schoolroom, giving
me, however, a half-angry, half-loving kiss
as she passed me, and saying:—

"Pale Ethel! if I were mamma I should
make you go to bed for the rest of the day.
Maggie's own nurse is quite enough to attend
to her."

But mamma was still full of the subject we
had been discussing, and on Gertrude's departure she asked me to repeat over again
exactly what I had heard; and then she took
it all to pieces, and examined every separate
bit with infinite relish—for having lived all
her life in a village, this good mother of mine
had a very fair appreciation of village dain-
ties, and never willingly threw away any that
were offered to her—and it was only when
she had tired herself out with suggestions
and conjectures (I will not say how soon she
had tired me) that she wound up by the
philosophical observation that after all it was
no concern of ours, and perhaps scarcely
respectful to our excellent vicar thus to map
out his future for him.

No concern indeed of ours—no concern
whatever of mine. So I kept repeating to
myself all that long afternoon, because I
suppose mamma's words had struck upon
some odd corner of my brain, and I was feeling tired and weak, and unable to do battle

with any stupid or ridiculous thought that might harass me with its continual presence. I read to Maggie again for some time, little story books of course, that had no interest for me, nor even the small merit of keeping my attention fixed on the incidents with which they were filled. I believed the day would never be over, the glaring sunshine never subside. It was an odd kind of relief to me when I was called down stairs about four o'clock to receive a visitor, mamma having gone out, and Gertrude never choosing to be interrupted in her duties with our pupils for anybody.

I have called it an odd kind of relief that I felt, because under all ordinary circumstances the person I was going to entertain was very far from agreeable to me, and even now I was tolerably sure that the interview would not have the effect of lessening the weight on my spirits from which I was suffering.

Mrs. Arnott (for that vivacious lady it was

who had done us the honour of calling) rose
on my entrance, and, assuming a sympathi-
sing look, in place of the free and easy one
which usually distinguished her, said she had
not been able to resist walking down to in-
quire after us all, and especially to know how
that dear child with the broken arm was
going on. She had been to the Miss Downings on her way, and heard as much as they
could tell her. She was so very sorry for
everybody, particularly she thought for poor
Miss Dora, whose marriage she supposed
would be delayed by this unfortunate event,
and who seemed really taking the matter as
seriously to heart as if Maggie were already
her own—so very flattering though to the
vicar, was it not? Poor man! he would
need some extra consolation in the trial of
having his darling laid up. Should we not
be greatly relieved when the child could be
removed to the vicarage? Mrs. Arnott had
heard that Mr. Wyke had consulted Mr. Luke
on the expediency of getting her home the

following day—he was naturally unwilling to give us the trouble of nursing her when we had our other pupils to look after, and the Miss Downings had kindly proposed taking it in turns to go and sit with the little invalid and amuse her.

To all of which I only replied that I considered Maggie no trouble, and should be glad to keep her as long as her father thought fit to trust her with me.

" So very kind and unselfish of you, I am sure, my dear ; but everybody knows you are one of the best creatures in the world. I am told that the vicar himself is quite fond of you ; looks upon you almost as his own daughter. How nice that is for you. Now I am sure, he positively dislikes poor me, though how I have offended him I cannot guess, unless it was that when he first came amongst us I tried to make myself particularly agreeable to him ; just for fun, you know, and certainly with no ulterior object ; for I would not marry such a grave, sanctimonious old

man for the world—oh, by-the-bye, what a
darling that Walter Kenyon is. I am over
head and ears in love with him, and shall take
some of the poison Susan keeps for rats, if I
can't make an impression on his heart. There
is a capital understanding of some kind between him and Lizzie Vivian—and oh, good
gracious! speaking of the Vivians reminds
me that I have such a piece of scandal for
you—at least, you virtuous people here will
doubtless call it scandal, though I firmly believe it to be true. Do appear a little interested, there's a dear girl, for it concerns
your cousin, Meta, most of all."

I was interested in a moment, even to the
length of asking this magpie of a widow to
tell me immediately to what she referred.

"Oh, I only had it this morning in a letter
from my cousin, who still corresponds with
Mrs. Vivian, and is intimately acquainted with
several of their friends. She says that the
Vivians and the Hallams were a great deal
together before both families went away for

the autumn, and that Miss Kauffman is
strongly suspected of being engaged in a de-
sign to win Edmund Hallam—the future Earl
of Clinton, remember, and the present Earl
lying dangerously ill—from poor Alicia Clarkson. Of course, it is a shameful thing, if
true, for I would back your cousin against
twenty such meek-spirited girls as Alicia, any
day. My correspondent adds that Edmund
has been seen with the Vivians at Brighton
more than once since they arrived there ; and
assuredly neither red-faced Mrs. Vivian, nor
her interesting offspring, can be the attraction.
What do you think of it ?"

In truth I thought a great deal more of it
than I chose to communicate to my gossiping
visitor. To her I only said that I would wait
for more definite information before condemn-
ing Meta, or pitying Alicia, and then, as
mamma, fortunately for me, came in, I escaped
for a few minutes to my own room, and, with
my aching head pressed against a cool pillow,

tried to reason myself into a sublime contempt for all that Mrs Arnott had been telling me.

It was not because I was unsuccessful in this that my tea proved as great a trial to me as my dinner had done. I was really very much worn out; and when Gertrude heard of Mrs. Arnott's long visit she said my loss of appetite was quite natural, and persuaded mamma not to press me to eat against my will.

They made me, however, lie down as soon as tea was over, promising that Maggie should not be neglected, and that if Mr Luke came, and had any special directions to give, I should be summoned to receive them. I did not like to ask Gertie to have me called when the vicar arrived, but I made sure that she would see to this herself, and so I yielded with no further reluctance to the physical prostration that must in the end have conquered me, and soon forgot, in a deep and dreamless sleep, every trial and vexation that the long day had brought me.

It was quite dark when I was roused suddenly by the opening of my door, and the sound of a cautious footstep advancing towards my bed. It was my mother, who had come to see if I still slept, and to ask me what I would take for supper.

"Has he been here?" I said, scarcely awake yet, but having a confused notion that they had suffered me to sleep too long.

"Mr. Luke? yes, my love; but he did not want you, and advised us by all means not to disturb you. Maggie is going on nicely, he says."

I had not meant Mr. Luke, but I allowed the mistake to pass, satisfied that mamma would tell me about the other in her own time. And presently, when I had assured her I was rested and was feeling better, she continued:—

"But we have had two other visitors, besides the doctor, to-night—Mr. Wyke and Mr. Kenyon. The vicar apologized for bringing his friend with him, but it seems he had wished particularly to come. They had a cup

of tea (for I had made some for Mr. Luke);
and then, while I took the vicar to Maggie,
Mr. Kenyon went out into the garden and
amused himself with the children. Gertie
did not seem to like it at first, and refused,
rather ungraciously I thought, to join them,
but Lizzie came in for her so many times,
that at last she did go, and they all stayed out
till the vicar sent to say he must be returning
home."

"Have they been long gone?" I asked.

"Not ten minutes. They both left their
compliments for you, and Mr. Wyke seemed
really grieved at hearing you were so tired.
By-the-bye, it is all settled for Maggie to be
taken home to-morrow. Mr. Luke says she
can be removed without the least difficulty,
and her father is naturally anxious to have her
with him. I don't fancy, though he has not
breathed a word on the subject, that he will
ever let her come to school again."

I had no excuse for remaining alone any
longer, so I asked mamma to send me a candle,

and having arranged my tumbled hair, and bathed my face in cold water, I went down stairs to take my usual place at the supper table, and to wonder what aspect life would wear to me when my little Maggie, who loved me, and whose love had been sweeter than I knew till now, was taken from me, and consigned wholly to the care of her future step-mother, Miss Dora Downing.

CHAPTER IX.

A SUNDAY AT THE VICARAGE.

MR. WYKE could not come to take Maggie home himself, having an unusual amount of parish work upon his hands that day, so for the present, at least, I was spared the grief of hearing from his own lips that my little pupil was to be no longer mine. Time enough for this communication when she should have so far recovered from the effects of her accident, as to make it possible for her to resume her school duties.

For the first few days succeeding her removal to the vicarage, we sent Betsy every evening to learn how she was going on, but as the reports were always satisfactory during that time, mamma thought it unnecessary to continue these frequent inquiries, and said she would call herself at the vicarage after church on Sunday, and take either Gertie or me with her.

"Let it be Ethel by all means," said my sister, who had been unusually affectionate to me of late, "Maggie would rather see her than any of us, and she does not dislike making visits as I do."

So mamma and I, without waiting that morning for the usual greetings at the church door, left my sister to return home with her pupils, and walked straight from the church to the vicarage. Mr. Wyke had not arrived when we got there—he generally had some poor person or other to go and see in the village after each service, and I often thought that Sunday was anything but a day of rest to him. Maggie's nurse admitted us, and then, rather to our surprise, followed us into

the drawing-room, closing the door carefully,
before she even asked us to sit down.

"You will excuse me, ma'am, I know,"
(this was to my mother), "when I tell you
what I have to say. One of the ladies from
the cottage is with the child now, so I shall
not be missed for a bit. The truth is" (and
now she turned to me), "the truth is, Miss,
I'm not at all easy about Miss Maggie's health.
It's quite true that the arm is going on all
right, and that the dear child makes no particular complaint, but for all that I don't like
the looks of her, and what I don't like in
them becomes plainer every day. I haven't
the courage to give even a hint to the vicar,
and the doctor he says, I am an old simpleton,
and talks about a shock to the nervous system
and so on. But, Miss, I saw that blessed
child's mother took ill and die, and if this
ain't the same complaint coming on I knows
nothing whatever of illnesses. I make so bold
as to speak to you, Miss, because I know you
are so fond of the poor lamb, as she is indeed

of you. The lady from the cottage—the one
as is with Missie now—is very kind and good
in coming to stay a bit with her sometimes,
but she's but a poor sick creature herself, and
I've never seen the good of talking to her
about it. I should be very glad if after you
and your ma have seen Miss Maggie and
noticed, as I am sure you will, the change in
her, you would try to say a word or two to
master just to warn him like—you ladies can
do things gentler and tenderer than we poor
people—of what may come to pass. Will
you be pleased to come up now to master's
study where she always lies on the sofa in
the day time, or will you take something first
after your walk, and wait for the vicar?"

While nurse spoke my heart had seemed
literally to die within me. If an oracle from
heaven had come suddenly and proclaimed
that Margaret Wyke must die, I don't think I
could have believed it more implicitly than I
believed it from listening to this poor ignorant
old woman's opinion. And strange to say I had

never calculated on such a possibility, in connection with Maggie's accident, before. I
had thought of a long, wearying illness; I
had thought even of an amputated right arm;
I had thought of shattered nerves that might
take months to be braced up again, but I had
never, never thought of death—death for his
darling, the light of his eyes, the desire of his
heart, the one solitary flower left to bloom
beside him in a bleak world and shed its sweet
fragrance on all the air he breathed. How
would he breathe, how would he live when it
was torn away from him!

"We had better go up at once, had we
not?" said my mother, startling me by the
calmness of her voice as she turned to address
me, after saying a few words—matter of
course, cold words, they seemed to me—to
poor nurse on the subject of her apprehensions—"the vicar may be late, and we must
get home for dinner."

I could not speak just yet, so I followed
the other two up-stairs, and then, when

mamma had gone into the study before me, I stopped for a moment, and by an impulse I could not resist shook old nurse's hand heartily.

" God bless you, miss," she said, with tears in her eyes—it was not for want of sympathy that there were none in mine— " I knew you would feel for us—and you will contrive, won't you, to speak a word by-and-bye to master ?"

" A hard task, nurse," I answered— " harder perhaps than you think, but I must see Maggie first. Don't you suppose it possible that you may be making too much of her symptoms ?"

An ominous shake of the head was all the reply I got to this, as the old woman retired from the door, leaving me to enter.

Predisposed as I was to receive an unfavorable impression, the first glance I had of the little white face laid against a pillow that seemed scarcely whiter, convinced me that nurse was only too correct in her suspicions.

Mamma stood, and Miss Dora sat with a book in her hand, beside the sofa on which the child was resting The former moved as I came in that Maggie might see who it was, without the trouble of rising. She did rise, however, the instant I was in sight, and, weak as she was, flew to me with every token of the most vivid pleasure.

"Oh, I wanted you so much (in a little eager, whispering voice), I have wanted you every day. Papa said you were too busy to come and see me—will you stay now—just for to-day—there is no work in your school on Sunday—do, do stay with me."

"My dearest Maggie," interposed Miss Dora, in a very kind, but as I thought authoritative voice—" you must come back to your sofa and keep quite still. Miss Ethel will, I am sure, sit beside you for a little while, as I must be returning home; but don't talk, there's a darling, to make your head ache, and I will come again to-morrow and read you a new story."

Now Maggie—like a few grown up women I have known—would obey instinctively whoever took the trouble to command her, but—like these women also—she would be quite incapable of loving the persons, however worthy, who by exacting her obedience called out and made prominent even to her own observation, the feeble points in her character. Its strength was its power of loving deeply, and joyfully sacrificing self for those it loved; its weakness was its exceeding timidity, which would ever incline or rather compel her to do, through the influence of fear, what love or a principle of duty should alone have had the right to suggest.

I knew by the change in her countenance as Miss Dora spoke, exactly what she felt, and so I took her up in my arms—she was but a light weight even then—and laid her myself with a shower of kisses on her sofa. I was just going to tell her I could not stay to-day, when mamma said—

" My dear Ethel, you are not really wanted

at home. If Maggie likes you to remain an hour or two with her, I am sure you had better do so. Nurse will bring you up something to eat that will keep you till tea time, and you can come home in the cool. What do you think of it?"

I had no opportunity of thinking anything of it, for Maggie's uninjured arm was clasped tightly round my neck, and she was declaring I should not go ; and by the time Miss Dora had got her bonnet and shawl on, the vicar had arrived, and somehow the matter was all settled for me, and mamma gone, before I was very clear as to what was really being asked of me.

Looking down upon his little daughter's pleased and happy face as she held my hand, and kept repeating again and again how very glad she was, it was perhaps not unnatural that the father should appear somewhat glad too. He thanked me very cordially for consenting to stay, though he must have known that my part had only been an unresisting one in the matter, and then he asked me (as if confident of a favourable reply) whether I did not think Maggie getting on rapidly.

This at least was not the moment, if indeed it should ever come to me, in which to arouse his fears about his darling, so I only said evasively that the arm seemed to be doing nicely, and that we must not look for much colour in the cheeks until she could run about and play in the open air again.

"My little Maggie!" he said then with that, ineffable tenderness which none but mothers are supposed to feel towards their children, but of which some few fathers are capable also; "my little Maggie, you must get well for poor papa's sake."

The words themselves were nothing, but the tone and the look that accompanied them made them most sadly, most passionately eloquent to my ear and heart. It was a relief to me when the vicar was soon after summoned to his dinner, and Maggie and myself left for awhile alone.

They sent our dinner up to us in the study, and the little invalid, charmed at an opportunity of playing the hostess, grew quite animated, and lost for the moment that pallid, fading aspect, which had so struck us when I first came in.

We had the vicar and Mr. Kenyon for half an hour after their dinner was over, and they both said how surprisingly well Maggie was looking to-day, and what a wonderful physician I must be. Walter Kenyon was very kind and affectionate in his manner to this sick child, and appeared to me altogether a different person from what he had ever done before. Had I met him now for the first time I should have judged him to be a particularly quiet, amiable, and even religiously disposed young man, for when the vicar spoke, as it was natural and fit for him to do, on matters adapted to the holy solemnity of the day, Mr. Kenyon responded with an intelligence and earnestness that not only looked like sincerity, but suggested a very warm personal interest in the subject discussed.

"Do you like that gentleman?" I asked of Maggie, when they had both left us for the afternoon service.

"Oh, so much," she replied instantly, "he comes and sits with me every day, and brings me often new books and toys from Boltby; and do you know, Miss Ethel, I think he is a good, good man."

By the double adjective, Maggie meant to express that she considered the person to whom she applied it religious. It was a curious fashion of her own, but one that always pleased me. In describing simply amiable individuals she would call them "good," but if she believed them to be religious like her father (I don't think, poor child! she had met with many besides him that she could have instanced as examples) then they were "good, good," and this highest of all compliments she now paid to Walter Kenyon.

When I enquired why she thought thus well of him, she could only say that he talked to her out of the Bible, and was papa's friend, and she believed papa never liked very much indeed any but " good, good people."

" Oh, Maggie, then he must like very few," I said, on the impulse of the moment, " for very few are good in that way. Some may indeed wish to be, but we must strive with our whole hearts and souls, before we can hope to get true wisdom."

" Yes, I know," Maggie said, with a sudden look of deep gravity appearing on her little face, adding presently, as that unchildlike expression passed, " I think the lady who was here this morning is trying to be good, good. Papa told me so, but you must not tell him again. She talks to him a good deal every time she comes, and he lends her books, and he says her bad health has brought her to think of these things."

I said (but blushed afterwards for my exceeding folly in saying it), " Then I suppose, Maggie, Miss Dora is one of the few persons that your papa likes very much indeed—is it so?"

"I don't know," replied Maggie, opening her eyes rather wide at my question, "but will you read to me a little now? I have made my head ache, as she said I should, by talking."

I read to her till she fell into a quiet sleep, and then, covering her up carefully with a shawl, and lingering a minute or two to look closely into the little pale features now that they were in a state of repose, I crept softly and sadly from the room to take one walk alone—the first I had taken for years—round the old vicarage garden.

It had been much changed and beautified since our time, but enough of its ancient fashion still remained to render it strangely and even painfully familiar to me. It cannot but be painful to come, after an interval of years, to a spot associated with innocent joys for ever gone, or friends of whom death has robbed us.

I meant to take one turn only. I had no intention whatever of staying until the rather depressed mood in which I had entered the garden should have been worked up by thoughts of the past (mingled with some real anxieties connected with the present) into a fit of passionate sadness that brought tears, such as I rarely shed, in its train, and made me feel as if it would be impossible for me to show myself again in the house that evening.

I had never calculated on the chance of meeting anybody here. I had no watch, and I supposed it an hour earlier than it really was, nearly an hour too soon for the church-goers to be back again.

So I wandered on in perfect security, aimless as to the paths I chose, and anxious only to have my unaccustomed moaning over, or to get away from the vicarage before its master should return to it.

The ghost of my dead father, of whom I had been thinking so much, could scarcely have startled me more than did the sudden appearance of Mr. Wyke, coming straight to meet me up a little avenue of arbutus trees that lay to the right of the large, square garden.

"You did not know that I had made an opening into the paddock at the other end, to shorten the road from the church." he said, as he approached me, taking no notice of my tear stained face. "I assure you I find it a great convenience, and the small space required for a path through the paddock does no injury to the cattle that graze there. Will you walk down and see it?"

While he spoke, and spoke too of such common-place things as paddocks and cattle, I had ample time to compose myself, and—though I could not get rid of the traces of tears which I knew my face must bear—to assume an aspect of partial serenity, and tutor my voice into conventional quietness.

" With pleasure," I said, taking the arm he offered. " I left Maggie asleep, and came out here on purpose to look at your garden. You keep it in admirable order."

" Pretty well. I am fond of gardening myself, you see. What do you think of my crop of standard pears? I am rather proud of them, I assure you."

For quite ten minutes he talked to me in this way, calling my attention to fruit, and vegetables, and shrubs, and meadow grass for cattle, till the calmness I had struggled so hard to feign became real, and I had nearly forgotten all the desolate and painful emotions that had been oppressing me when I first met him.

Then, suddenly, as we were passing a fine old walnut tree, with a bench round it (we had often had our tea there in the old times), he said, in quite a different tone of voice from that in which he had been hitherto speaking to me:

" Sit down here for a little now, and rest

yourself—and, if it will not agitate you again, tell me what was grieving you so deeply half an hour ago."

The kind, kind voice, the gentle manner, the anxious look! how could I resist them? And yet I knew not how to answer him, how to reduce to words all the strange, sad, yearning thoughts and memories, which had been rushing through heart and brain since I came into the vicarage garden. At length I said, stupidly enough :

" Indeed I should be sorry to inflict on you or on anyone the sombre fancies that visited me, unbidden, this evening. I never thought to be detected in my weak indulgence of them. Will you forget all about it, and trust to my promise of being wiser for the future ?"

" That would be scarcely wise on my part," he said with half a smile, "inasmuch as my experience has been larger than yours in respect of the futility of *any* human promises —but at least tell me one thing—was it the past you were mourning over, the past which this afternoon spent in your old home brought back to you, or had thoughts in reference to the present or the future made the sun seem dark to you for awhile?"

"I am afraid," I acknowledged, "that past, present, and future, had each a share in my sadness; but it is over now, indeed it is, Mr. Wyke, and I would much rather not talk about it. Thank you, though, none the less for all your kindness to me. I wish I could deserve it or repay it better."

I know my voice was a little unsteady as I said this; but I hoped he had not noticed it. For a full minute he made no reply, then it was:—

"My dear child, if I could be ten times kinder to you than I am I should only be pleasing myself, and there would therefore be no merit in it, nothing deserving of thanks. Maggie does not thank me for being kind to her. I wish from my heart I could really serve you."

This last clause was spoken more earnestly,

more gravely, more thoughtfully that what had preceded it. I could not help suspecting that he referred to those matters which I had once so shrunk from his discussing with me. Even now the colour came into my face, and my heart beat quicker than usual as I said :—

"I have kept the promise I made you of reading to myself the Bible chapters which I have afterwards made Maggie read to me. I do not find it wearisome now."

"Thank God," he uttered in a low, earnest voice, seeming unmindful of my presence for the moment—then, abruptly turning towards me a countenance beaming with satisfaction, he added, "I should never be afraid of trusting you with any gloomy thoughts or anxieties if I could be assured that you had the One Friend to bear them *with* you who has already borne them *for* you, at least if you are on His side. Ethel, if I had an angel's tongue and could tell you what a world it is in which your lot is cast, what a nature it is with which you have to struggle against this evil world, you would at least believe in the necessity for seeking better help and guidance than the tenderest, truest, most devoted human friend could give you."

"I do believe in it now, but I am so weak, so ignorant, so full of errors of every kind. I love the world too, and the things that are in the world. How am I to help this?"

"You cannot help it, my child, but you can tell your trouble to the Friend I have been speaking of. Don't imagine because I am double your age and you deem me a religious man, nor even because I am a minister of the gospel, that I can help you the very least in the world. Trust to no arm of flesh, lean upon no human reed, strive not to quench your thirst at any tributary stream. You may, by asking, have the arm of Omnipotence to support you, and the one pure fountain of living waters to drink from—but if you continue to read His word, God himself will teach you all this, and more. May His blessing evermore be upon you."

It was very sweet and soothing to listen to such words as these from the lips of the friend I esteemed above all the world. An indescribable calm fell upon me as I sat there beside him in the still, fair, autumn evening, realising the privilege and happiness of his friendship, and wishing that time would not move on for a little while that I might drain to the dregs this cup of full contentment. I did not forget for a moment the possible bitterness in store for him, but in the lull of all stormy emotions which had followed the late storm of my soul I persuaded myself that it was only possible, not even probable, and that it would be both unnecessary and cruel to do poor nurse's errand to-night.

So, when our more serious converse was over, I spoke to him of Walter Kenyon, and asked if he shared his little daughter's opinion about this young man; if he was satisfied now that the early promise was being fulfilled, and his friend really walking in the paths he had formerly believed him to have chosen. I did not scruple to add that I was more than ordinarily interested in the matter from a belief growing upon me that he admired my sister, and was endeavouring to win her regard.

Very gravely, and I could almost fancy reluctantly, Mr. Wyke replied:

"I find Walter Kenyon still a professor of religion, and as such, unless his conduct gives the lie to his professions, I am bound to honour and esteem him. His volunteering to pay me a visit seemed to indicate that the world which undoubtedly courts him had not obtained any serious hold of his affections. Lately I have certainly thought that he might have some attraction in the neighbourhood. My suspicion was directed towards Miss Vivian, though I was puzzled too, she being but a child. Your sister would indeed be far more likely to have struck him, but I am sorry, while I stand in doubt of him, that you have good reasons for believing it to be so. If he is not what he professes to be, he must be worthless altogether. So clever too, so agreeable, so apparently kind and tender of heart! I should be deeply, deeply pained, to discover that this young man was only fair to the outside view. You saw him with Maggie to-day; you heard him talk to me. Does he seem to you otherwise than true coin?"

"I liked him to-day exceedingly. I could not believe any ill of him if he appeared to me often under the same favourable aspect. But there are some people who can be holy with the holy, and unrighteous with the wicked. I do not say or even think it is thus with Mr. Kenyon; I am only anxious to have him proved honest and true on my dear Gertie's account."

"You will see him again at tea to-night. We shall have our evening meal in the study with you and Maggie if you do not object. Walter went for a walk after church, but he will be in by six. Are you tired of the garden now?"

"No, but I must go home before tea—
mamma will expect me. I will just run and
give Maggie a kiss if she is awake, and then
get ready for my walk. It is long after five."

As Maggie was still asleep I put on my
bonnet without disturbing her, and on
descending into the hall found the vicar waiting, hat and stick in hand, to accompany me
hom .

I suppose I did not protest very vehemently
against this new instance of kindness on his
part, for he never for a moment relinquished
his intention, and it was certainly the happiest
walk I had, up to that time, ever had in my
life.

Only just before we came to Lindenhurst,
my exultation received a little check, by his
saying in the most hopeful tones:

"You will try to come and have another
look at your little pupil during the week, and
next week I trust, if she goes on improving,
there may be a chance of her getting to school
again."

Not even the satisfaction I was conscious of
in thus learning that he had never thought of
taking my darling and his darling away from
me, could lessen the keenness of the pang
that shot through my heart at the confident,
undoubting manner in which he seemed to
anticipate her complete recovery.

I felt then that I ought to have paved the
way, at least, for speaking to him openly of
nurse's fears—that I had been both cowardly
and selfish in avoiding all mention of Maggie's
health that evening. It was too late now,
for we were standing and saying good bye
at the gate of my own home, and while his
last low, fervent " God bless you !" rang in my
ears, I was again in great danger of forgetting
everything but the speaker of those three
little words which have been sometimes known
to stir the heart more than any other human
words have ever done.

CHAPTER X.

NURSE'S ERRAND EXECUTED.

As mamma told me she had not thought of mentioning to Gertrude the conversation we had had with nurse on the subject of Maggie's illness, I resolved that for the present I would keep silence, too.   My sister had not yet forgiven the little Munroes for their disobedience in the matter of the swing, and though she rarely alluded now to the accident which had been the result of this disobedience, I felt sure that it was often in her mind, and that she continued to blame herself severely for her forgetfulness of the child on the night of the calamity.

Early in the week succeeding the memo-
rable Sunday I have just described, as my
sister and myself sat in the schoolroom
together after the children had been dismissed to the garden till tea time, Gertrude
suddenly startled me, by saying :—

"Ethel, do you still think there is any
truth in the report about the vicar and Miss
Dora ?"

I looked up from a French composition of
Jane Norton's which I was correcting, and
replied that I did not really know. She was
certainly a great deal at the vicarage, took a
warm interest in Maggie, &c., &c.

"She would scarcely be a great deal at
the vicarage if she were engaged to the
vicar," persisted Gertie, to whom the idea of
this marriage was evidently not agreeable;
"and as for her interest in Maggie, she is not
singular in that; Maggie is a child to interest
most people.   When are you going to see
her again, Ethel ?"

"Mamma and I talk of walking down after

tea this evening. I have only heard of her through Jane since Sunday. Poor darling! I wish we could see her back in her place again. Without Maggie I have not half enough to do—you take so much the largest share of the work, Ethel."

My sister did not reply to this, but she ceased writing abruptly, and leant her arms on the table before her, seeming to have got hold of some disturbing subject of thought.

I said again, with a view of rousing her:—

"I wonder whether we shall hear of any more pupils after Michaelmas. Mrs. Vivian promised to do her best for us, did she not?"

"Ethel, our school will not succeed!" This was spoken quickly, and decisively, and in a voice suggestive of intense despondency—"I feel quite certain of it; all the hopes with which I commenced working are gone; my energy is fast going; the children we have at present do not satisfy me—they are not real workers; they have no ambition. Even Lizzie Vivian has her head full of a hundred things that ought never to have come into it till her education was completed. I thought young people would be more easily managed. I expected that I should be able to form their minds in some measure, as well as put knowledge into their heads. I am disappointed in everything, Ethel, and whether we get other pupils or not, I feel persuaded that, as I understand the word success, this school of ours, round which I built such magnificent hopes, will not succeed."

It occurred to me to wonder, as Gertie thus sadly and bitterly spoke, whether the discovery of her own heart being less under her control than she had once deemed it, had anything to do with the disappointment and discouragement she complained of.

But I only said, as cheerfully as I could :—

"You take extreme views of things, dear. Maggie's accident occurring here has for the time upset us all, and it is perhaps not unnatural that you should feel especial resentment at a disobedience which led to so disastrous a consequence, but, after all, children like Fanny and Louisa will be thoughtless and wilful at times; and had Maggie not fallen from the swing, we should have given them some slight punishment, and then have forgotten that they had transgressed our orders in putting her into it. As for Lizzie Vivian, I fancied you had been hitherto tolerably content with her."

"I am learning more of her," said my sister, shortly, "and I don't expect she will bring me much credit or satisfaction in any way."

Just then we were called down to tea, and during the short time we were together afterwards, our conversation was not resumed.

It was to please me, I know, that mamma had agreed to go that evening to the vicarage. She had seen how anxious I was about Maggie, and, though thinking nothing herself of nurse's fears, she sympathised sufficiently with my uneasiness to make a sacrifice of her own convenience on my account.

" It will really be a good thing," she said, as we walked and chatted together, " when Miss Dora gets settled at the Vicarage. A child like Maggie wants a closer looking after than the best of fathers can give; and I firmly believe that Miss Dora will be perfectly well and strong herself the moment she has somebody else to think of. These nervous women are more benefited by working for others than by all the medicines in the world."

To which I assented, venturing however to add that I did not think we had sufficient grounds for crediting Mrs. Arnott's report, to speak of it as a settled thing."

" Why, my dear child," said mamma almost indignantly (for having made up her own mind on the subject, ever since the day of the widow's visit, she did not at all admire being told she might be wrong;) " you must be blind, indeed, if you did not observe how completely Miss Dora seemed at home in the vicarage study on Sunday, with what authority she spoke to Maggie, and how, in every way, she showed her consciousness of having a right, superior to ours, in the house that was soon to be her own."

I did not think it necessary to tell mamma then, that I believed she had imagined at least half of this. If I had my own private reasons for doubting that the vicar was going to be married, I had also the common sense to know that I might be mistaken in these reasons, attaching to them greater importance than they merited, and deluding myself with notions that would turn out to be less substantial than air. At present, but for the turn mamma had given the conversation, my mind would not have been occupied with the question of marriage at all, for I had resolved, if after seeing Maggie and speaking again to nurse, I found that necessity existed, I had resolved, I say, at any cost of pain to myself

—and it *would* be most cruel pain to wound my best friend—to break to Mr. Wyke his old servant's apprehensions on the subject of his daughter.

We found Maggie downstairs on a sofa, by an open window of the sunny parlour, and Walter Kenyon reading to her. The vicar was not at home, but they expected him every minute; in the meanwhile my little friend was pleased and grateful that I had come so soon again to see her; she had not expected me for several days; she was growing dull and tired in having nothing to do, and should be so glad to get out and come to school once more.

I thought as she spoke that these must be good signs, and I drew aside the curtain shading the window that I might have a better view of her face, which had become a little flushed on our entrance. Alas! the closer inspection was far from satisfactory; there was a loss of flesh even since Sunday, a deepening of the purple under the eye, a sicklier tinge on the fair skin, an increase of lines round the small mouth, and altog ther a growing look of unearthliness, if I may so express what I mean —that made me tremble as I gazed at her.

Walter Kenyon caught my eye as I withdrew it from its pained observation, and by a very slight but expressive shake of the head convinced me that he, at least, understood and shared my fears. Presently, when I had gone to the other end of the room to lay aside my bonnet, he followed me, and told me, in a low voice, that he was beginning to think badly of Maggie's health; also that nurse had been speaking to him.

"And the father," I said anxiously, with a sudden hope that my dreaded task might be spared me—"has anybody hinted yet to him that there may be danger—does he see it for himself?"

"Not a bit, and nobody in the house will ever, I am sure, have courage enough to enlighten him. Frankly, I could not do it, knowing how dear that child is to him. Mr.

Luke too, I verily believe, pretends that there is nothing amiss only to have an excuse for putting off the announcement of it to the poor vicar. He is so much beloved, you see, that nobody can endure to give him pain—such pain especially as that would be—but I fancy nurse said something about *your* having promised to do it."

"I did not promise," I answered with a sick and sinking heart—"but I will try what I can do rather than suffer him to remain in ignorance till the last. Such a blow falling abruptly might kill him."

"It will not come far short of that in any case," said Walter feelingly, "I would give a few years of my own life very cheerfully to save Mr. Wyke from this sorrow. He is a good, noble-hearted, admirable man."

I made a mental note of this warm eulogium for future remembrance, but at present the vicar occupied all my thoughts, and on Mr. Kenyon saying:

"Why not go and meet him in the garden?

he is sure to come in that way," I went out at once, with a fixed, though sorrowful, determination to do what was expected of me, before any fresh instance of the father's love and confidence could be brought before me, to weaken the very little courage I had been able to muster for the occasion.

I waited at the paddock gate for at least a quarter of an hour—growing of course more nervous every minute—before he was even in sight. Then, when he came near enough for me to see his face distinctly, the tired, worn look I could plainly trace in it, awakened my tenderest sympathy, and made me shrink a thousand times more than ever from the idea of saying a word to him on the miserable subject, to-night.

He seemed a little surprised, but then pleased, I thought, to find who it was waiting for him.

"Thank you," he said, taking the hand I extended and not immediately relinquishing it, "for you have come, I know, to pay another visit to my poor little girl, and your coming is such a real joy to her. Are you well yourself?"

"Quite well—but you, Mr. Wyke, I don't think you are very well—you look so tired."

"I am not tired now, Ethel," he replied with a smile that would have made me supremely happy but for the terrible duty which lay before me, "still I shall not object to rest for a few minutes on the seat under the walnut tree that you know of. Will you stay with me?"

"Yes, if you like—"

I could not get beyond those four words, and even they seemed as if they would choke me in their utterance. Why did he not ask me the reason of my being at the gate to meet him, anything to form an opening to the dreaded disclosure I was there to make.

But my quivering voice had struck him, and, as he drew my arm tenderly within his own, he glanced quickly into my face—that I thought would tell no tales—and said:

"Something ails you again to-night, Ethel;
I begin to fear the vicarage garden has a fatal
influence over you. Won't you confide in me
even yet?"

" It is not the vicarage garden," I stammered
out in desperation at last, "and it is not
about myself at all. Mr. Wyke, I *must* tell
you—because you ought to know, and because
nobody else will tell you—that we all think
Maggie in worse health than you believe.
Nurse spoke to me about it on Sunday, and I
ought to have broken it to you then, only I
was trying to hope she was wrong, and it
seemed so dreadful to give you pain. Mr.
Kenyon has mentioned it to me this evening,
and I have seen and judged for myself. I
came out on purpose to meet you and say all
this. I could not do it better; it hurts me
so very much to have to do such a thing at
all. I hope—"

At this point of, surely, the most awkward
speech that, under similar circumstances, was
ever uttered, I broke down entirely, and

should have sobbed aloud but for the dread I had of increasing his distress, and obliging him to attend to me when all his thoughts and anxieties were so imperatively claimed in a more legitimate quarter.

He did not say a single word until, with the utmost gentleness, he had seated me on the bench before alluded to, and taken a place beside me. Then, having given me a little time to grow calm—perhaps requiring that time to grow calm himself—he drew both my trembling hands into his, and said :

" My child, I know what this has cost you, and I thank you accordingly. The thought has come to me before, Ethel, often—often—scarcely the fear, because I would not entertain the thought till it should grow into this. God is the best judge of what I need, and He holds the universe in His hand. Will you go in now to Maggie, and leave me to follow presently. I will come soon, Ethel, I will indeed."

This last must have been in answer to the half frightened, appealing glance I turned towards him, as, in instant obedience to his request, I rose from my seat and prepared to leave him.

To leave him alone in his great sorrow or, at the least, in his great fear, not to dare to breathe a single word of sympathy, or comfort, or affection, that might have fallen like gentle rain upon the fever of his heart, and, in some very slight degree, have mitigated its anguish.

This was hard—this was torturing—and yet it was most natural and fit that he should wish to be quite alone during his first surprised communings with the "strange thing," that he was told was coming upon him. What could I be to him at such a moment? What had I expected to be?

I was turning away with swimming eyes and bursting heart, after he had spoken those last words, when some sudden instinct seemed to reveal to him my feelings.

"Ethel," he said again, and now I detected an indescribable weariness as well as sadness in his voice. "Ethel, my child, you must not be grieved that I send you from me for a while. If any human being could help or comfort or bless me in this hour, it would be yourself. Now, go."

And I went, creeping into the house with slow and mournful steps, as if I had committed some guilty act in thus bringing sorrow and dread into the heart of the good man whose tenderness for the sorrows of all around him, had made him beloved and honoured in no common degree.

Nurse, who had evidently been on the watch ever since my arrival, met me in the passage, and entreated me to tell her what I had done. Briefly and tearfully I communicated the little there was to hear, and begged the old woman, who was crying too, not to show her own grief in the presence of her master, but to comfort and support and cheer him all she could.

"God bless him!" she exclaimed, with a
fresh burst of tears; "he knows I'd give my
life for him, or for that precious lamb either;
but it's small comfort I shall be able to bring
him when that blow falls. The Lord he
loves and serves must do it all; but it's my
belief He'll do it by calling him to follow his
darling."

Not greatly cheered by this myself, I went
on to the room where I had left my mother,
and explained to her as well as I could in a
hurried whisper, while Walter amused Maggie,
the cause of my absence. She could not make
any comment then, as nearly at the same moment the vicar entered—very, very pale, but
calm as I had ever seen him, and quite alive
to the duties of a courteous host, as he manifested by his kind reception of my mother.

He had been quite five minutes in the
room before he approached his little daughter's sofa; then he only bent over her with a
kiss and a few tender words, and as mamma
was now talking of our going home, turned

and proposed to walk part of the way with us.

"I have to see Mr. Luke to-night," he said quietly, when we protested against his leaving home again; but though he insisted, tired as he was, on conducting us to our own door, he made no other allusion during the long walk to the one painful subject which was occupying all our thoughts, and none who knew him superficially would have guessed by the composed, agreeable, almost cheerful tone of his conversation, that on his heart to-night was laid that bitterness with which, no less than with some certain special joys, the stranger intermeddleth not.

CHAPTER XI.

MR. LUKE'S EARLY VISIT.

WE were sitting at breakfast the next morning when Mr. Luke was suddenly ushered in ; he had not ten minutes to stay, he told Betsy, and would not trouble the ladies to leave the table on his account.

"A case up in the fields, about half a mile from your place, has brought me out at this unseasonable hour," he explained, as we gave him a chair, and mamma pressed coffee and toast upon him. " I thought I would not go by your very door without stepping in to say ' how do you do,' and to tell you that there's

a pretty kettle of fish to fry up at the vicarage,
where some wise-acre or other has been putting
it into the parson's head that his little girl's
going to die. He swears—at least he doesn't
swear, because he's a good man—but he pro-
tests that it is not that old fool of a nurse, of
whom, mind you, I have nevertheless very
strong suspicions. He came to me last night
full of mild reproach for what he termed my
want of candour, and though nobody likes to
be blamed unjustly, or taken to task for a
fault they have not committed, I really forgot
to be indignant on my own account, in my
sincere pity for the man's grief which he was
bearing so bravely and manfully. Hang it!
though I've been a doctor these five and
twenty years, and seen care and sorrow
enough to kill half an empire, it cuts me up
like a woman to witness some kinds of mental suffering. Our vicar has got too tender a
heart for the world we live in. One would
have thought his duties, as a clergyman,
would have brought him in contact with

enough of sadness and tears without having
his own home invaded by them. But, at
least, those croaking old women—nurse, or
the Miss Downings, or somebody, might have
let him rest in peace and quietness for as
long as it was possible. *I* have never said
the girl must die, and I suppose I am, at any
rate in Graybourne, the best authority."

As the little doctor never once paused
during the above rather lengthy and animated
speech, I had no opportunity of putting in a
word till he came to the end, and was swal-
lowing, at frightful risks, a cup of boiling
coffee that my sister had just handed to him.

Now, I said as composedly as I could—
feeling the whole matter so strongly :

" I was the croaking old woman, Mr.
Luke, who warned the vicar of Maggie's
danger. I thought it right and kind to do
so, believing, as I cannot help doing, that
danger to be unmistakeable. Nurse and Mr.
Kenyon, who live in the house with her, both
see it plainly, and Mr. Kenyon is under the

impression that you purposely shut your eyes to the fact from the dread of having to give pain to the vicar. What you have now said appears rather to justify this notion, therefore if you have really the least idea that the child is seriously ill, I am sure in your heart you must be grateful to me for what I have done. It was not a pleasant task, I assure you."

Mr. Luke, who had grown rather red and extremely fidgetty during my explanation, jumped up abruptly from his chair as I ceased speaking, and walked to the window. My sister, who now for the first time heard Maggie's danger alluded to, became very pale, and turned instinctively towards Fanny and Louisa upon which, both those unhappy children (understanding of course that the accident in the swing was the sole origin of their little playmate's illness) burst into tears, and rushed, without even asking permission, from the room.

"God bless my soul!" exclaimed the poor doctor, as Gertrude, with a most ominous gloom upon her face, was preparing to follow them. "I had better not have come here at all this morning, for it seems I am doing nothing but mischief. Pray, Miss Beamish," (this was to my sister), "make use of your own excellent judgment in this unfortunate matter, and don't imagine for a moment, nor let those frightened little girls imagine, that if the vicar's child goes into a decline, the broken arm has had anything to do with it. The mother died of consumption, you know, and Margaret has always been of a consumptive tendency. I tell you all, once more, that I see no absolute reason for dooming her to death even now. She has no cough, and her increasing thinness and paleness are only the natural result of her nerves being shaken, and the absence of her usual exercise. I have told the vicar as much (bless your hearts! I couldn't have helped giving him

some little comfort in the state he was in
last night), and I have advised him to send
or take her away to the sea-side for a month.
Now, my good Miss Ethel, let me earnestly
advise you not to alarm him again at present,
and not to listen yourself to that silly old
nurse's whinings on the subject. The child,
it appears, is fond of you; not such bad
taste on her part; go and see her as often as
you can; get her into the garden; keep her
mind amused; and by and bye we shall see
how things will turn out. Old port wine,
cod liver oil, meat three times a day; we'll
give her all this, and, we'll hope for the best.
Good morning, ladies."

I think he was not sorry to get away, for
indeed, he must have felt, in spite of his own
determination to look on the bright side of
the painful subject he had been discussing,
that we were the last people to whom any
mention of it could be welcome. Say what
he might, through kindness to us, or through

choosing to maintain his first opinion, we could not help believing that the accident had at least hastened the development of those symptoms in poor little Maggie, which were beginning so seriously to alarm all interested in her.

My mother certainly endeavoured, after Mr. Luke was gone, to impress us with the idea that he had spoken from conviction, and that his opinion, as a doctor, ought to carry some weight with it; but I believe she only did this because she saw how Gertrude took the matter to heart, and that having made her own observations the evening before, while I was in the garden, she was in reality quite inclined to view the case as gloomily as I did.

My sister said very little, either now, or afterwards when she was alone with me, on the subject; only her countenance and manner testified to the deep concern with which the intelligence about our little pupil had

filled her; and as I was going into the school-
room with her on the ringing of the bell that
summoned the children from the garden, she
turned to me and entreated that I would
leave all the teaching to her, and walk down
to the vicarage, as Mr. Luke had advised, and
stay with Maggie.

"Miss Dora will be there to-day," I
replied, "and one companion at a time
is quite enough for the child. Besides,
Gertie, I should not choose to leave you
while you are so depressed. I wish, dear,
you would not keep all your gloomy
thoughts to yourself; they become infinitely gloomier from being unshared, I
assure you."

"Possibly, Ethel," she said, "but it is weak
to cry out for sympathy and pity the moment
anything has hurt you. This has never been
my habit, as you know. Whatever I may
have to bear, I can certainly bear alone. We
must not, however, waste any more time in

talking here. You will surely go to the
vicarage in the evening?"

"Unless we send. I don't want Mr.
Wyke to grow tired at the sight of me."

Again Gertrude turned quickly towards
me, and this time with something almost approaching a smile on her lips. She made no
further remark, however, and we both went
then into the school-room.

I am afraid there was not much good done
either in the way of teaching or learning that
morning. Mr. Luke's visit had put all ideas
in connection with the acquirement of useful
knowledge out of all our heads. Fanny and
Louisa had cried till they were quite sick; and
although Gertrude conscientiously repeated to
them what the doctor had said about the accident having nothing to do with Maggie's
present symptoms, I could not help feeling
that her tone and look, as she fulfilled this
duty, was not greatly calculated to raise the
crushed spirits of the little delinquents.

When Jane Norton came I asked her if her
Aunt Dora had gone to the vicarage, and on
her reply in the affirmative, I enquired
further what the Miss Downings thought of
Maggie's health, for hitherto—not caring particularly to have the result of any more of
Jane's observations on the subject of her
youngest aunt's matrimonial hopes—I had
not even mentioned to her my own fears concerning the child, nor alluded to the vicar's
household in any way.

"Aunty Dora never talks much at home
about her visits to Maggie," Jane said, in
reply to my question; "I don't think she considers the little thing seriously ill, but she
has often remarked that she wants a mother
to look after her." Then in a whisper —"I
know Aunt Harriet believes that this will
soon be brought about, and she is nearly as
pleased and happy for her sister, as she is
for herself—you know what I mean, and he
comes to tea twice every week now, and we

begin to look upon him as quite one of the family."

Jane was not remarkably clear in her communications to-day; but, had she been far more so, I could scarcely have felt interested in them. My heart was heavier than those around me guessed, and though I would not go to the vicarage I would have given worlds to have seen Mr. Wyke, even for one minute —to have been assured that he was not yet utterly crushed by the grief he was bearing, as Mr. Luke had said, "so bravely and manfully."

In the evening, when weary of the long day and of my efforts for Gertrude's sake to appear cheerful, I had strolled out to the front gate to watch for the return of the messenger we had sent to the vicarage, the friend who was engrossing all my thoughts suddenly came himself, and stood on the outer side of the iron gate in front of me.

Before I had time even to ask after Maggie,

or to utter one word of kindly greeting, he said :—

"Will you fetch your bonnet, Ethel, and come into the fields with me for half-an-hour? I want to talk to you."

CHAPTER XII.

SUNLIGHT IN THE FIELDS.

"Do tell me something of Maggie," I entreated, as, having joined the vicar, who insisted on waiting for me at the gate, I was walking beside him towards the fields he had spoken of. "We had sent Betsy to the vicarage, you know, and I was watching for her when you came up."

"You are very good to take so much interest in my little girl," he said, offering me

his arm now, as if the idea had just occurred
to him—"and I promise you that I shall have
talked quite enough about her before our
walk is over. . She seems to me the same as
usual to-day, though, having had my attention
called to it, I must confess that her thinness
has struck me more than it ever did before.
She *is* very thin and very pale, certainly—
but I saw Mr. Luke last night, and he is less
despairing about her than you and nurse are,
Ethel. He is of opinion that change of air
may do wonders for her yet. I shall take her
to the sea-side as soon as I can get a friend I
know to come and to do my duty here for a
month or two. What do you think of this
plan?"

" It is a very good one, no doubt, especially
if Maggie herself appears to like the thoughts
of it. I have seen Mr. Luke also, and he told
me it was most essential to keep her mind
amused and interested. Of course there will
be plenty at the sea-side to amuse and interest her."

" So I should imagine. I mentioned the subject to her this morning, for I dreamt all night, you see, of the doctor's suggestion, catching at it as drowning wretches catch at any stray plank that holds out a hope of rescue for them. I wanted to discover how the prospect pleased her."

" Well," I said anxiously, though something unusual in his manner—something which gave me the notion of a deeper vein of anguish than the surface showed underlying that calm exterior—made the father even more than the daughter the subject of my anxiety—" well, and what was the result?"

" I will tell you when we get into the fields," he replied ; and again his tone struck me as peculiar. " If I am walking too fast for you, stop me—my thoughts travel rapidly to-night, and like many solitary people I have acquired a habit of walking and thinking to the same measure. But perhaps you are tired."

" No, not physically tired. My mind was

growing very weary when you arrived. I
have not had a moment's peace since last
night, since I spoke to you in the garden, and
stabbed you as cruelly as your bitterest
enemy could have done. Of course I meant
to do rightly and kindly, but it was an un-
gracious office I assumed; and—and I don't
believe you will ever like me again."

Why I said this, and said it, as I am sure
I did, in a tone of almost passionate complaint, I could never tell. It is true I felt it,
and had been feeling it keenly and bitterly
from the moment Mr. Wyke had offered me
his arm that evening; but when I commenced
the speech which terminated in those excited
words, I had not the faintest intention of
uttering them, or even of alluding to my unhappy impression in any way.

I was terribly ashamed of myself, miserably
confused and abashed when the thing was
done, and when in the silence which succeeded,
I had leisure to reflect on my folly. Was

this a time to dwell on any personal emotions or fancies whatever, when the friend beside me was threatened with one of the heaviest griefs the human heart can suffer, and when the most distant echo of its far off footsteps was even now crushing his brave spirit to the earth? Oh, mean, little, selfish that I had shown myself! what should I be to him henceforth?

Although the silence was painful, I had not the courage to speak again till I had heard his voice, and could judge as to the *degree* of contempt my weakness had inspired. But at least seven or eight minutes must have elapsed before there was any other sound than the nervous beating of my heart, and the rustling of the tall elm trees that skirted the road along which we were walking.

Then we had reached the fields; and my companion, having made me pass before him through a narrow gate into a pathway where the evening sun was shedding down a flood of

golden light, came once more and placed himself beside me, and drew my arm with the old
tenderness that I recognized—oh, so thank-
fully and joyfully, through his own.

"Ethel," he said, in a low but perfectly
distinct and impressive voice—"you must
disown the words you just now uttered. You
must never, never think such hard thoughts
of me again. I am going to prove to you how
hard and erroneous they were, by asking you
to be my wife, by telling you, child, that you
are dearer and more precious to me than anything in the wide world, and that my greatest
fear, my greatest anxiety at this moment is
that you should reply 'I can give you all
esteem, but I cannot love you.' Ethel, I may
be thought too old, too grave, too saddened a
man to be a fit husband for a girl like you,
but I love you as younger men perhaps
rarely love, and I would not have you for a
wife unless you could love me a little in
return. This is what I brought you into the

fields to say. Can you answer me now, or
must I give you time to question your heart
and conscience on the subject?"

In recalling (as I have sought to do in writing this history), with the most faithful
accuracy, every impression and emotion of
which I was conscious on that eventful evening, I can think of no words that do not
appear hacknied and commonplace that
would describe the feelings with which I
received this, my first offer of marriage, from
the man whose friendship alone I had deemed
of more value than any other possession I
supposed it possible for life ever to bestow
upon me.

For a few seconds after his voice had
ceased, I think my brain was dizzy from
the weight of unutterable gladness pres-
sing on my heart. I did not want to
show this in its extent—not yet at any rate,
but it seemed too vast to be hidden—where
should I put it out of sight? I looked down

at the golden mist streaming across our path, and for no reason that I knew of, my eyes suddenly overflowed with tears. I was afraid that he would misunderstand them, that he would think I cried because I had only esteem to offer him. It seemed to me now. that henceforth my one great object in life must be to add to his happiness, never for a single instant voluntarily to cause him pain. He had seen my tears, he had taken my hand gently, caressingly, encouragingly in his own, and he was going to speak again, when, looking up with momentary courage into the kind, kind eyes that would never, I knew, have grown less kind to me, had I spoken far other words, I said :—

" If you take me for your wife, you shall be satisfied with your wife's love for you. It is all I have to give, so in this one offering I may well afford to be generous."

He believed me, and he thanked me ; and I am sure for those few first minutes, after we had thus shown each other what was in our hearts, after we had become convinced that those hearts for weal and for woe were for ever united, nothing, nothing,—either in the past, present, or future,—came with the faintest shadow athwart the full and perfect brightness of our mutual joy.

My Harold, my love, my husband! It is something to me still to know that once— even for that brief, brief period—I was the means of raising to your lips, a draught of life's richest, purest, sweetest wine, the taste of which lingered with you and mingled somewhat, as you have ever assured me, with the bitter and heart-sickening potion that later days had in store for you.

*   *   *   *

We talked, at length, when all the golden sunlight had deserted our fields, and the damp autumn twilight was wrapping them in gloom, of our sick darling at the vicarage,

and of the doctor's idea of sending her to the
sea-side.   Then it was that the father told
me, smiling gladly now, as he knew what I
should say to it, that on his mentioning the
plan to Maggie, she had declared she should
only like to go if I would go with them, and
that he had promised her to see if he could
not bring this about.

" So, Ethel, dearest," he continued, turning for about the twentieth time in the
pride of his new privilege, to draw my shawl
closer round me, " you must suffer me to be as
good as my word to our poor little drooping
flower, who needs the sunshine of your continual presence to warm her into active life
again.   You must put no unnecessary obsta-
cles in the way of our marriage, but let it be
accomplished speedily, that we may take
Maggie away and have our own holiday,
before the later and colder autumn days set
in."

When I had quite recovered the breath of

which this startling proposition had deprived me—it is one thing to be asked to marry a man at some indefinite time, and another thing to find out that because you have said 'yes,' you are expected to give up your freedom immediately. When I say I had quite recovered my lost breath, I answered jestingly:

"Oh, then, it is on Maggie's account, and because that dear child wants to have me at the sea-side with her, that you have requested me to become your wife. It is very good and self-denying of you, Mr. Wyke, but under the circumstances I think I must retract my promise of marrying you. Maggie shall not, however, be disappointed. I will go with her still, but it shall be as her friend and governess."

If even then, beneath the light tone and the glad, buoyant feelings with which I thus spoke, there lurked some hidden seeds of jealousy and mistrust, I was at least unaware of their existence. The words—such idle

words as we often utter, and think no more
of—had been suggested by what the vicar
told me of his little daughter's wish in reference to myself; but at that time, with my
whole heart and soul filled with the one idea
of his entire and perfect love for me, it would
have been impossible for me to have had any
conscious emotion of doubt or fear corres-
ponding to the words.

Neither did it occur to him, in his own
grand, simple, absolute faith, both in himself
and me, as regarded our love for each other,
that I could really mean what I had so
thoughtlessly spoken. He replied therefore
lightly to my accusation, deeming that it
needed no serious denial, and again recurred
to the subject I had as yet evaded—namely,
the expediency of our being married as soon
as possible.

I will not weary my reader by dwelling on
the many things, some wise, but more foolish,
I have no doubt, that I said in reply to his

arguments in favour of his own plan. Suffice
it that the result was my consenting (on the
condition of mamma's approval), to do all
that he wished, even though this might entail
the necessity of my leaving Gertrude unpro-
vided with an assistant in my place, and—
graver still—the being married without a
bride's complete outfit.

As this last thought crossed my mind, I
suddenly remembered poor Miss Dora, whose
trousseau was supposed to be arriving in
weekly instalments from ready made linen
warehouses in London, and once more I was
tempted to jest a little with the friend whose
dignity had been laid so gracefully and
graciously at my unworthy feet.

"By the bye," I exclaimed, as we came
near home, and would in a few minutes have
to part—"I am afraid I have supplanted
another lady who had good reasons—so say
all the village—for believing herself the future
mistress of the vicarage. You know you have

for a long time been paying most unreasonable visits at a certain cottage, and if I did not think it would make you vain, I would tell you how much and often I have pondered on the daily increasing friendliness between you and Miss Dora Downing."

"Child, child!" he cried, drawing me to his heart and kissing me (he would not jest any more to-night). "I am sure I did not so skilfully conceal my love for yourself, even when, in its first birth, I deemed it an old man's folly, that you should have ever suspected me of bestowing it elsewhere. I will talk to you of Miss Dora another time—now it is very late, and the night air is chill and unhealthy. My darling must go in."

And so we parted ; but for that one night I determined after his last tender farewell had ceased to vibrate in my ear, to listen voluntarily to no other human voice. For just a little while I must keep to myself the treasure of my vast gladness and pride, I must fold it close to my heart of hearts and learn to look at it in a humble as well as in a thankful spirit.   By and bye it might be easy to say to those around me, " Come and see to what a lofty and undeserved height this good man's love has raised me," but now—for to-night— I must wear my crown of beauty, my royal diadem, alone, with no mortal eye either to admire or depreciate its splendour.

I will try though, to hold it, at length, meekly in my hand, and to bow with it in praise and gratitude before the throne of that gracious Father, who has chosen for me as protector, guide, and husband, a man walking in the fear of the Lord, a Christian Israelite in whom there is no guile.

CHAPTER XIII.

ANNOUNCING MY ENGAGEMENT.

I STOOD by my mother's bedside at a very early hour on the following morning. I had not been able to sleep since it was light, and knowing that mamma generally awoke with the first streak of dawn, I thought this would be a good time for making my important disclosure, and for apologising for having shut myself in my own room on my return from the fields last night.

"My dear Ethel, what are you doing out

of bed so early?   You will disturb the rest of
the house, and Gertie sat up with me rather
late yesterday evening, and will be tired.   I
am glad you have come to my room, though,
for I wanted to say a word to you about your
staying out so late with Mr. Wyke.   Had it
been anybody else, my dear—I mean any
other gentleman—I should really have been
seriously annoyed.   Of course the vicar is a
perfectly safe person for a young lady to be
trusted with, but upon my word, Ethel, I am
not sure, in spite of your being so much
younger than himself, that Miss Dora would
quite like it."

This was the morning greeting I received
from my dear, prudent mother, who, I am
afraid, had been awake even earlier than
usual, brooding uneasily over her daughter's
strange conduct, and perhaps attributing to
the good vicar something short of perfect
fealty towards the lady on whom the village
had decided he should bestow his hand.

Notwithstanding the rebuke thus abruptly administered to me, I bent smilingly down when the speaker had concluded, and kissed her on both cheeks.

" Dearest mamma, the question I think is not so much whether Miss Dora would like it or not, as whether you will like it—will like to have the vicar of Graybourne for a son-in-law, and to see one of your daughters mistress in our dear old home. Mamma," (and now I hid my face as I told the rest), " he has asked me to be his wife, and I have consented; and I am very, very happy, for I love him dearly, and think there is no one like him in the whole world."

When I looked up again after thus explicitly stating both my position and my sentiments, mamma was rubbing her eyes very hard indeed—no doubt with the object of discovering whether she was awake or asleep. At length she said :—

" I don't think you are joking, Ethel, but I

feel there is a mistake somewhere. It is impossible that so good a man as Mr. Wyke can have asked you to marry him, when we know he is on the point of marriage with Miss Dora Downing. You must have dreamt this, my dear, or have misunderstood something he had said to you. Besides, you are really but a child, compared to the vicar, though of course he is very far from an old man yet. What did he say to you, my love?"

" Just what I have told you, mamma, and a great deal more that I shall not readily forget. If you think it so strange that he should love me—I feel, indeed, I am quite unworthy of his love—at least give him credit for knowing his own mind. He is coming after breakfast to see you, and perhaps when he himself tells you what I have told you, you will believe it. I am sorry you should not be able to believe me."

I was a little indignant, and I showed it, because I thought this might help to convince

my incredulous listener of the truth of the
assertions I had made. She sat up in bed
now, and looked me earnestly in the face for
about a minute without speaking. Then suddenly she put her motherly arms round my
neck, shed a few tears, and blessed me as
heartily and affectionately as I could have
desired.

"My Ethel must forgive me," she said, as
I returned her caresses—"it seemed too good
news to be true. There is no one in the
world to whom I could so cordially entrust
one of my dear girls as to Mr. Wyke. Your
poor father would have been proud and glad
of such a husband for you. But how could I
think, my child, that he had any idea of you
as a wife, when it seemed so clear that he had
chosen Miss Dora. You must explain this to
me, Ethel, for I cannot understand it even
yet."

"Nor I, mamma, quite," I answered laughingly—"so I believe you must be content to

wait till the vicar comes, and you get an explanation from him. I want to go to Gertie now, that I may not hinder her while she is dressing. Say you are pleased, dear mother, once more."

She said it with additional emphasis, several times more, kissed me again and yet again, and let me from her most reluctantly at last, that I might make Gertrude a sharer in our gladness. My sister was not incredulous as mamma had been. On the contrary she declared she had long suspected that it would end in this—she had seen that the vicar liked me more than others, and she had believed lately that I was beginning to care for him.

" But are you quite, quite sure that you are happy, Ethel dearest ?" she asked, as I knelt beside her bed with her hands clasped in mine—" that it is not from a wish to have a home of your own, to be a mother to Maggie, or to escape from this teaching drudgery, that

you have accepted Mr. Wyke. Marriage
you know, dear, is far too serious a thing to
be entered upon with doubtful motives—
with—"

" Oh Gertie, Gertie, don't go on," I interrupted with almost choking emotion—" it is
dishonouring to him even to suggest the possibility of my accepting the gift of his dear
love without returning it. I do love him,
Gertie, with my entire heart and soul, and if
he were homeless and houseless to-morrow,
I should be but too thankful to share his fate,
and to dedicate my poor life to his happiness."

" Then," said Gertrude, kissing me nearly
as fondly as mamma had done — " may
Heaven's blessing be upon you both; and it
surely will, Ethel, for if you love the man
you are going to marry, there is no single
advantage wanting that I can see to the
union. I am so glad to know that my dear,
dear sister will have a happy life."

The words as well as the tone were to my ears painfully suggestive of other expectations for herself; and folding my arms tightly round her, not looking into her face to embarrass her by what I was going to say, I whispered coaxingly:

"Tell me, darling, why you have been less happy of late than you used to be. Do tell me, now that you know my secret, what is on your mind, Gertie?"

She put aside, with quite as much firmness as gentleness, the arms in which I had imprisoned her, and replied coldly—she could be cold even at that moment.

"Ethel, I have nothing to tell. We are all greatly distressed about Maggie, and I have mentioned to you before that the school has disappointed me. There are no secrets to be given in exchange for yours. The bell has rung, I believe, so you must go now, dear, and let me get up."

I obeyed her, and spent the remainder of

the time before breakfast in looking up all
Maggie's books and other scholastic property,
making them into a parcel to be sent to the
vicarage. I knew now that she would come
to school no more.

The children had been dismissed from the
breakfast table, and mamma, Gertie, and
myself were just drawing our chairs together,
in preparation for a family gossip, when a
certain vigorous ring at the garden gate sent
the blood dancing from my heart to my face,
and caused an interchange of smiles (why
will lookers on always smile on these occasions?) between my two companions.

Guessing that my friend, if it were he,
would like to see me first, I quietly slipped
out of the room, without any explanation,
and ran, before Betsy could get from the
kitchen, down the pathway to the gate.

I was not disappointed, though the strange
feeling (which I had not calculated upon) of
meeting by broad daylight, for the first time

L 5

as a lover, this grave, dignified vicar, who
was really, as he had once said, double my
own age, almost took my breath away as I
came up to him, and made my cheeks a crimson flame.

The shy man, whose shyness I had formerly
so often laughed at, had assuredly the best of
it now. Having once shown me his heart,
and become convinced that mine was wholly
in his keeping, there was no room in that
simple, noble nature, for embarrassment of
any kind as far as *I* was concerned. He
greeted me with the fondest of smiles, and, as
soon as I had opened the gate for him, bent
down and kissed me as composedly as if this
had been a life-long privilege.

"Are you in the habit of acting as por-
tress, Ethel?" he asked; "or did you guess
that I should be so early a visitor?"

"Oh, I knew it was you," I said, regaining
a little self-possession now, and anxious to
punish him for appearing so much more at

his ease than I had done ; " of course I was
quite certain that you would be here as soon
as you had a hope of gaining admittance,
and I came to let you in because—"

I could not immediately think of anything
sufficiently uncomplimentary wherewith to
wind up my revengeful speech. Had my
lips proclaimed that I had been in no hurry
to see him, I am afraid my face would have
given them the lie. As I paused and tried
to look very calm and indifferent, my companion smilingly took up my broken sentence.

" You came, dear, because your heart inclined you to come, and mine has bid you
welcome. This is just the sunbeam that I
needed—to warm and cheer me for the long
day. We won't go into the house for a
few minutes, Ethel. If you do not fear
taking cold without your shawl, we will
have a turn in the garden first."

I feared nothing with him ; so we went

round the lawn to the wilderness side, and
as we walked he told me that Maggie knew
of what he was pleased, in his great kindness, to call "the happiness in store for
her," and that she was nearly wild with
delight.

"Stepmothers are not usually welcomed
so enthusiastically," I said, while a glow of
thankfulness and joy warmed my heart in
reflecting that I might really be a blessing to
this dear child; "but I shall hope, with
God's help and yours, to be a mother indeed to our darling."

"My dearest," he said, "you know I have
unbounded faith in you, in your love for both
of us. It seems to me that when I have you
with us, Maggie *must* get well. She looked
so bright and happy this morning when I
went to her bedside and told her that Miss
Ethel was coming to live for good at the
vicarage as her mamma. By the bye, I
promised her to bring you back with me; we

must get your sister to give herself a holiday
for once, and come too, Ethel. I am sure
Mrs. Beamish will undertake the charge of
your young ladies, and perhaps bring them
all to tea in the evening. We will have it
under your old walnut tree, and you shall
preside as mistress of the ceremonies. Now
don't say one word against my plan, for
indeed I have quite set my heart upon it, and
so has Maggie. I cannot do without my
darling to-day."

It was worth something to see the grave,
bashful, reserved vicar of Graybourne coming
out in so new a character; acknowledging
thirst for companionship, suggesting *al fresco*
entertainments at the vicarage, and making
projects for his own and his daughter's
amusement like any ordinary mortal.

Truly the change I had been the means of
working in this friend of mine would have
filled my heart with pride, but that his love
which gave birth to the transformation had

already made me, in the consciousness of my undesert, so very humble.

Of course to the vicar's tempting invitation I replied that I should like nothing better, if he could manage it with mamma and Gertie; and soon after this we went into the house, he to have his interview with my mother, and I to find my sister, and coax her, if it were possible, into going with me to spend the day at the vicarage.

The bell had not yet summoned the children into the school-room, and Gertrude was sitting there alone, waiting patiently for the daily drudgery—I did not forget that for the first time she had herself called it drudgery that morning—to begin.

I went up to her, all glowing from my happy walk in the garden, and made my petition, not without many doubts and misgivings as to how it might be received.

"It is the vicar's first request to you, dear," I whispered as I saw the sudden red mounting into her cheek, and a look of steady resistance taking possession of her whole countenance, " don't refuse him, Gertie—it will seem so hard, and unkind."

" I daresay I am hard and unkind, Ethel," she replied, in a voice that chilled me, " but I cannot help it; I am as nature made me, and I fear I shall not improve as time goes on."

" No, no, my darling," I cried, embracing her against her will; " you are not as nature made you, when you look and speak as you are doing now. Nature made you sweet, and loving, and gentle, and womanly, and you are seeking to mar her handiwork. This must not go on, Gertie—I cannot endure to see it. You exclude yourself from everything which other girls find pleasure in—you lead a hermit's life, without the hope of a hermit's reward—you take up the martyr's cross, without any reference to the martyr's crown. Gertrude, my dear, dear sister, I cannot be

happy myself and not passionately desire to
see you happy too. Come with me for this
one day to the vicarage. It is not asking
much—is it?" Look how the sun is shining,
and hear how the birds are singing, and put
your head out of that window and breathe
for a moment the fresh, lovely, exquisite
autumn air. Ah, you cannot still say no;
you will come for my sake."

" Who are surely happy enough just now
to dispense with such a small addition as this
concession on my part would make to your
happiness," she said in a gentler tone, and
stroking the hand I had laid on her lap.
" Dear Ethel, do believe that your great
gladness makes me glad."

Then for a few minutes she sat quite still,
looking at the waving trees outside the
school-room window, and at the sunshine that
came dancing in and playing on the uncar-
peted floor, and finally at the scattered books
and slates, and portfolios, in which presently

she must concentrate all her interest again if she continued to refuse my request.

An expression that I did not understand, but which appeared to me almost defiant— defiant perhaps of some feeling by which she refused to be conquered—was on my sister's face, as she suddenly turned it to mine and said:

"Ethel, you have won the day. The children shall have a holiday in honour of your engagement, and, if mamma will take charge of them, I will go with you to the vicarage."

CHAPTER XIV.

A WHITE DAY.

I VERILY believe that if our dear, kind mother had been asked to stand upon her head, she would have tried, under the circumstances, to accomplish the feat, rather than have deprived Mr. Wyke of the pleasure of taking us back with him to the vicarage.

I had not time to ask her much about her interview with her future son-in-law, because when I went down to them in the breakfast

room to announce Gertie's decision, he
entreated that we would get ready at once,
that he might return to the village and finish
his work there as soon as possible. Only
while he was shaking hands with my sister,
when we were both dressed, mamma con-
trived to draw me a little aside, and whisper
to me :

" There was never a word of truth in the
report about Miss Dora ; but, my dear, I had
no conception that Mr. Wyke wanted to take
you from me so soon ; we shall not have half
enough time to get your things made. Do
you know he says it must be in a month at
latest."

" Now, Ethel," called out Gertrude from
the other end of the room, before I could
reply, except by a heightened colour, to what
mamma had said to me, " We are keeping
Mr. Wyke, and mamma too has no time to lose
if she is to look after those children till the
evening."

" I am quite ready," I said, walking over
to where Mr. Wyke and Gertie stood, and not
sorry to escape any further questioning just
then, " Is it settled for mamma and the rest
to come to tea?"

" Quite settled," answered the vicar, with
an animation that I saw astonished my sister,
" and Miss Gertrude has been promising me
to lay aside all anxiety till she sees her pupils
again. She looks as if she had sat too much
in the school-room of late, and I want her,
even more than you, Ethel, to have a thorough
holiday."

Perhaps he knew that the sunshine in my
heart would make it holiday for me wherever
I might pass the next few hours, and whether
I worked or rested.

My sister was undoubtedly pleased and
touched by the vicar's kindness, and either
out of gratitude to him, or because, having
once cast off the yoke, she was determined to
enjoy her freedom to the utmost—from one or

both of these causes her spirits rose from the
moment we left the house, and it gladdened
me inexpressibly to hear her talking freely
and cheerfully with the friend who very properly neglected me a little during our walk,
that he might the more exclusively devote
himself to her, and thus prove that he appreciated the effort she had made in our
favour.

I lingered behind them several times
intentionally, and once, feeling rather weary
from my nearly sleepless night, I sat down for
a few minutes on a bank by the road side,
thinking as they were walking slowly that I
might soon overtake them.

There was a gate leading into some of our
fields close behind me, and before I had been
seated many seconds I heard a man's lively
whistle and immediately after a rapid footstep
coming up the path to the gate I have
mentioned. I should have decided that it
was the vicar's guest, but that Mr. Wyke had

told me he was gone out fishing for the day, and would not be back till quite late in the evening.

I turned round with some curiosity (for gentlemen who whistled operatic airs with skill and sweetness were not common in Graybourne) in time to witness a very light and graceful vaulting over the low barred gate, and to receive the cordial though astonished salutation of Mr. Walter Kenyon.

" It's too warm and clear a day for the fish to bite," he said, in reply to my enquiry about his angling expedition, " so I left all my tackle at a cottage by the trout stream I had an order for, and was coming home for my sketch book to see if I could amuse myself for an hour or two in that way. You have seen the vicar this morning."

" Yes," I was obliged to acknowledge ; "he came to ask my sister and myself to spend the day at the vicarage. Maggie is dull when her father is obliged to be out, and—and Mr. Wyke and my sister are just in advance of me now. I sat here to rest for a minute."

His face expressed the most undoubted satisfaction, as I gave him this intelligence. " I hope," he said, " the vicar won't send me away again if I go home now. Oh, how grateful I shall feel evermore to those most sensible fish if I am allowed to remain and spend the day with you young ladies."

"And in the evening mamma is coming with our pupils to tea. You will have an opportunity of seeing Miss Vivian."

" Thank you," he replied, believing, I suppose, that I was quizzing him ; " I don't know that I particularly care about that. But won't you accept the help of my arm now, and come on after your companions. The vicar will think something has happened to you."

In which it seemed that Mr. Kenyon had guessed correctly, for as I rose to do as he suggested, wondering how Gertie would like the addition to our party, Mr. Wyke suddenly appeared in the distance, coming very fast and alone in a backward direction.

We walked rapidly enough towards him for my increase of colour to have a natural explanation. Mr. Kenyon hastened to say how he had found me resting on the bank, while the vicar very quietly took my arm, which the other had relinquished, and drew it, in an appropriating manner that the dullest looker on must have understood, through his own.

I saw Walter's face assume an expression of rather surprised intelligence ; then he half smiled to himself and said aloud—

"As you have apparently left one lady, Mr. Wyke, to come and look after another, had I not better run on and assure Miss Beamish of her sister's safety. Miss Ethel is a little tired, and cannot walk very fast."

" Miss Beamish is resting also," the vicar replied, " but you can precede us if you please, Walter. I will take charge of Ethel, now."

He did not wait for a second permission, but walked off with a speed that in a few minutes conveyed him, as the road was winding at this point, quite out of sight.

"What *will* Gertie say?" was my first exclamation on finding myself alone with the vicar; "it will be such a surprise to her."

But he was not thinking of Gertie or of Walter just now.

"My child, you should not have lingered so far behind. I was afraid you were hurt at my neglecting you for your sister. There went a sharp, sudden pain through my heart when I thought I had caused you one instant's pain, my darling. But it was not this, was it? You were only tired and staying to rest yourself."

" That was all indeed," I said earnestly, and feeling more and more subdued at every new proof of his love for me. " I was so glad to see you and Gertie getting on well together; I never could have felt that you were neglecting me. I was very, very happy—as I am now, Mr. Wyke—when I sat down on that sunny bank and watched you walking on in advance of me."

"My own Ethel," he answered in a voice whose unfathomable tenderness sank down deep, deep into my heart; " you cannot guess what it is to me to hear you say you are happy, and to believe that I have been in any degree the cause of your happiness. I shall have urgent need to watch and pray that I may not make an idol of this treasure that God has given me."

Presently he added, as I could not speak just then for the emotion that was nearly choking me.

"But how long, my dearest, am I to be Mr. Wyke to you? Do you consider me too old or too grave to be called by my christian name? I want you to feel quite at home with me at once, Ethel, and I want all around us to understand that you are marrying me because you like me."

" As if I could hide that, even if I wished it," I said eagerly (for did not his great and generous love deserve the fullest return that I could make to it?) " but I think if I ventured to call you by your christian name just yet, I should feel I had committed some awful act of presumption the next time I saw you in your pulpit, with that stiff and formidable and awe-inspiring black gown on."

He laughed at this as I intended him to do, for we were now within sight of my sister and her companion, and I had no fancy for being detected by them in a sentimental mood, or for exposing my friend to the possible ridicule of Mr. Walter Kenyon. In the few minutes that we had still together before reaching the spot where they waited for us, I told Mr. Wyke how it was that his guest had not stayed at the trout stream, and what he had said about hoping he might not be turned adrift again.

"I shall have no excuse for sending him away against his will," the vicar said reflectively, "but depend upon it, Ethel, however much he may admire your sister, her exceeding dignity and coldness will keep him at a safe distance. Are you very tired now, love?"

"Oh I am not tired at all; our talk has quite rested me. Let us make haste on to Maggie now."

Gertrude was not looking, when we joined her, as if the apparition of Mr. Kenyon had produced any very alarming effect upon her. He smiled very kindly at me and hoped I had got on better since Mr. Wyke had come back to give me the support of his arm. Then we all proceeded at a quicker pace to the village, where the vicar left us, at our request, to hasten over his parish duties, while we

went on, with our other escort, to the
vicarage.

*   *   *   *   *

Amongst the many, many happy days—
for every one of which I desire to be deeply
grateful—that my life has known and that
memory still fondly chronicles, there is none
that stands out more prominently, or round
which imagination delights more frequently
to linger, than this one which I am now going
very briefly to write about.

I will not dwell on Maggie's joyous and
loving reception of me as her future mother.
I had long known how the child had attached
herself to me, and I was prepared for her
innocent and demonstrative gladness on the
occasion. Gertrude left us together for a few
minutes just at first, and by the time she
joined us I had calmed down the somewhat
wild spirits of the little invalid to a gentle,
satisfied contentment, that was much better

for her in her weak state than the feverish excitement she had been disposed to manifest.

My own cup of thankfulness and joy overflowed when, later in the morning (my sister having accepted Mr. Kenyon's invitation to walk with him round the garden), the father came in, and finding Maggie on my knee, wound his arms tightly round us both, and blessed us, leaving his hand tenderly pressed on my head after he had withdrawn it from his little daughter's.

Ah! I did not doubt then that in his heart's sanctuary of hidden treasures I was the first and the dearest. The vast love wherewith I loved him exacted nothing less than this, but rested in a sweet, full, calm assurance that this was mine.

We sat together—we three—in a happy, delicious communion of thought and feeling that needed few words to express its blessedness, till somebody came in to scatter the

golden sunbeam that had been bathing us all
in its light, by the very prosaic announcement that dinner was ready, and that Mrs.
Luke (who had been invited partly for the
sake of her matronhood, and partly, I verily
believe, that the news of our engagement
might be circulated through the village), was
with Miss Beamish in the garden.

I thought when I saw Walter and Gertie
that they must have had a happy morning,
too, and I could not but be glad, without for
once looking on anxiously into the future.
Perhaps I was beginning to think with
Maggie that her father's friendship for this
young man was a guarantee of his worthi-
ness. Certainly I was convinced that none
but the most utterly reprobate could dwell
long with the vicar of Graybourne without
coming to esteem goodness and holiness as
the fairest things on earth.

We were a very cheerful, sociable party at
dinner, during which the master of the house

took care that everybody should clearly
understand the position I occupied towards
him. It was not by any ostentatious attentions that would have embarrassed me that he
did this, but by the lower and softer tone
when he addressed me, the gentler and more
familiar look when he glanced towards me,
the nameless something in the whole manner
by which a man who is truly attached, pro-
claims instinctively, in reference to the chosen
object, " behold my love." That Mrs. Luke
was both astonished and mystified I clearly
saw, but she was a plain, matter-of-fact
woman, and would not trouble herself long—
not nearly so long as mamma had done—
about the question of Miss Dora's prior claim.

Mr. Wyke told us before we left the table
that both the sisters from the cottage with
their niece, Miss Norton, were coming to tea ;
also that Miss Dora would sit with Maggie
during the afternoon, as he had ordered
carriages to take the rest of us to Beechwood,

Mrs. Hallam having left an order for his general admittance, with what friends he pleased, to the park and gardens during her absence.

This was the little treat he had planned, as he subsequently told me, in especial reference to Gertie, because he was sure she did not allow herself sufficient change and recreation for her health and spirits. And I thought more of it, and loved him better for it, than if he had done it on my account alone.

The kind, kind heart, the generous spirit! when were they not employed in devising good, or pleasure, or help, or profit, for some one?

We had two large open carriages, the first containing Mrs. Luke, Mr. Kenyon, Gertie, and Miss Downing; the second, only the vicar, Jane Norton, and myself.

I need scarcely say that it took that acute young lady but a marvellously short time to discover the error she had lately committed

in assigning Mr. Wyke to her aunt Dora. I
was infinitely amused at her startled look
when she first heard my friend address me by
my christian name, with a little adjective
tacked to it that there was no mistaking.
After this, she discreetly busied herself in
admiring every detail of the landscape, or in
straining her eye to catch a glimpse of the
carriage in advance of ours. Occasionally,
I saw her give herself a little hug, as if she
was both pleased and entertained ; but upon
the whole we could not have had a better
behaved companion, and I gave Mr. Wyke
great credit for having selected Jane as our
third.

Once arrived at Beechwood she joined herself to the other detachment, and as it was
agreed that everybody was to be free for the
next two hours to wander whithersoever they
pleased, meeting again on the lawn at half-
past four, we saw nothing of her, or indeed
of any of our party, during that interval.

Mr. Wyke took me to the woods—brown, golden, and crimson now with their autumn foliage—where we had walked for a little while together on the day of the Beechwood fête. It was very sweet to us both to recal that bright summer morning, and to assure each other that even then we had been conscious of some hidden sympathy lessening the distance that age and position and conventionality had outwardly established between us. Then, too, I had felt glad and joyous and happy, but it only resembled the gladness and joyousness and happiness of the present hour, as the first faint, amber light in the morning sky, resembles the full, golden splendour of the meridian day.

But we talked of many things besides our mutual love and mutual contentment, exhaust-less though these themes as yet appeared to be. I told him what I had heard about Meta and Edmund Hallam, and it was a relief to my own mind when he declared his utter in-

credulity of the fickleness attributed to the latter. "Of your cousin," he said (and I felt then the old burden of Meta's secret beginning to weigh upon me afresh), "I, of course, know nothing, nor very much of Edmund Hallam, but that any man who had once attached himself to so sweet a girl as Alicia Clarkson, could be won from her by a mere coquette, however accomplished, I will not for a moment believe. Besides, what motive could Miss Kauffman have in seeking to win an engaged person? Even Mrs. Arnott's vanity I fancy would stop short of this."

"It may be," I said, "that Meta is ambitious—and she knows that the Earl of Clinton is dangerously ill."

"The Earl of Clinton!" the vicar repeated with a sudden increase of interest that puzzled me, "what connection is there between the Earl of Clinton and the Hallams, Ethel?"

"Is it possible you do not know? But I

remember you told us, on your first arrival at Graybourne, you never asked questions about anybody, and gossip is as distasteful to you as to my sister. Well, then, let me be your informant for once, as this does seem to interest you a little. Edmund Hallam has become heir to the earldom we are speaking of, through the death, some four years ago, of a cousin who was descended in a more direct line from the Clintons, but who died unmarried. The Hallams have never spoken much of this themselves, and I am not really sure that it is at all generally known. It was Alicia herself, I believe, who told me, and until now I have never mentioned it beyond our own family."

"Ethel," said my companion, after a silence of a minute or two, and speaking as abruptly as if he had not been listening to my explanation, "do you really think there is a chance of this dangerous cousin of yours being engaged in the scheme attributed to her, and incited to

as I had ever that tender, loving voice, to encourage and applaud me in all I did, or failed to do ; ever those kind, kind eyes, to seek me out, and smile their gladness and their fondness into mine each time that such refreshment for my growing weariness was needed.

One privilege alone (to which I had been uninvited), I claimed for myself, and would not be denied, though Mr. Wyke pleaded that our holiday was nearly over, and that it was unfair to rob him of the smallest portion of it. Nevertheless, when I saw that Maggie was tired, and pale as a snow-drop, even in the midst of her pleasure and excitement, I insisted on taking her to bed myself, and remaining with her to read and talk (as I meant always to do by and bye), till she dropped asleep, happy and content as children with loving mothers should ever be.

Then it was, while I sat by my darling's bed, singing at her request a little simple

child's hymn to her, that old nurse crept
softly in, and told me by her kind, honest
face (before she could speak a word), that she
knew and rejoiced in what was going to happen to her master.

"For, if ever," she said, winding up thus a
somewhat lengthy address of hearty congratu-
lation, that for all its blunt simplicity affected
me to tears; "if ever there lived a blessed
man upon the face of this sinful world, that
man, miss, is the one you're going to have for
a husband; and I believe if ever there was a
lady likely to make him happy, and comfort
him when the great trouble that he won't see
comes down like a thunderbolt upon him, that
lady's yourself. May the God above bless
you both, and give you many, many happy
years together."

After this came a little more cheerful talk,
for those who were tired of the garden, in the
vicarage parlour. (I remember noticing that
Gertrude and Walter Kenyon were amongst

the last to come in), and then there was the
long, quiet walk home in the cool starlight
night, when once more my friend could assert
his sole right to me, and we could speak together as freely and unrestrainedly as in the
Beechwood grounds.

Mr. Kenyon took charge of my sister and
Lizzie Vivian, and mamma and the other
children brought up the rear.

Not until we stood before our own gate,
and the last lingering "good-night" had been
spoken, was I conscious of any perceptible
diminution of the gladness which all day long
had been overflowing my heart. It was not
that the parting saddened me, for I knew we
should meet on the morrow, and ere many
more morrows had winged their flight, that
we should meet to part no more till death
divided us—but it was a sudden feeling, or
rather instinct, that seemed to come to me
with a warning voice, bidding me be grateful
for, and make the most of, this bright and

blessed day, now gone for ever, because life had few such to bestow, and after so full a tide of unsullied joy there must come some dark, counteracting waves of trouble or sadness.

CHAPTER XV.

MRS. VIVIAN'S LETTER.

IT was not my sister's custom to come into my room before she went down-stairs in the morning. Except the day after the party at Fell House, when she came to announce to me the promise of a new pupil, I don't remember that she had ever so favoured me since our school commenced. I was therefore rather taken by surprise when the morning following our happy day at the vicarage, she claimed admittance to my sanctuary some time before I was dressed, and asked quite meekly if she should disturb me.

"The truth is," she continued when I had replied eagerly in the negative, "I am so unaccustomed to a whole day's idleness such as I had yesterday that it has made me feel restless and unsettled. I slept indifferently, and I am by no means in a working mood this morning. I will take no more holidays for myself, Ethel—they do not agree with me."

"Oh nonsense, Gertie," I said laughing, "I am sure you appeared very happy yesterday, and happiness must agree with everybody. Mr. Wyke was so pleased to think you enjoyed yourself."

"And indeed, Ethel, I felt his kindness deeply, as I should have done had it succeeded less in its generous object--but I did enjoy it all, Beechwood especially—thoroughly, and I want you to tell him so from me."

" I will, dear, though I don't see why you cannot tell him yourself. He would like you to feel completely at home with him, to look upon him in short, as—as a brother."

" Don't blush at that word, Ethel," she said gravely, " or at what it implies. You have every reason to be proud of Mr. Wyke's affection, and I have every reason to be grateful to you for giving me such a brother. But you know, dear, I don't get to be very intimate with people so easily as you do, and I want you, not only to thank him for me for his great kindness of yesterday, but to convince him that holidays are not necessary for me, that I have work to do which must be done, and that in fact (you must put this nicely and graciously, Ethel), that I am better let alone—do you understand?"

I think I understood her better than she supposed or intended, but I only said :

" Gertie, I won't give any such message, for I don't consider that you are better let

alone, or that holidays are unnecessary for
you. As for the work that must be done, it
will never be well done if you go at it like a
galley slave. Remember the old saying,
' All work and no play made Jack a dull
boy.' "

" But I am not Jack, Ethel," she replied,
with a seriousness that quite upset my gravity,
" I am a woman with woman's work to do,
and while conscious of a great deal of weakness I have still too much contempt for that
weakness to let it turn me aside from the
path I have mapped out for myself and mean
to follow to the end. I may not be able to
keep a school, but I will teach, I will labour
with the talents God has given me, I will do
some good in the world. Girls like Lizzie
Vivian may take the pleasure, may bathe in
the honey-dew of life, but mine, as I ever
foresaw, is a different mission, a different
destiny. I shall be the more content with it
the more I succeed in closing my eyes to all

others. If you really love me you will suffer me to please myself."

" Gertie," I said abruptly, so abruptly that my sister had no time to fashion an evasive answer, "how did you amuse yourself at Beechwood yesterday? Who had you for a companion, and what did you do?"

The bright red mounted to her cheek— possibly indignation at my questioning might have had some part in bringing it there— as she replied:

" More than half the time I was with the friends you and the vicar deserted. For a little while I was alone with Mr. Kenyon; he had brought a book, and he read to me while I rested. The other ladies are better walkers than I am, and they wanted to go every-where."

" What did he read?" I continued piti-lessly, ' Locke on the human understanding,' ' Mason on self-knowledge,' ' Hints on the proper cultivation of the mind,' or anything in that style, Gertie? You would of course have enlightened him as to your severe taste in literature."

"He read Tennyson's and Longfellow's poems," she said, with a quiet dignity that was doubtless meant to rebuke my sarcasm, "a style of reading better suited to the time and place than the works you have mentioned, Ethel. I have not the bad taste to dislike poetry like that."

"Oh indeed," I thought to myself as immediately after she rose and went out of the room, "and I wonder how far the inspirer of this improved taste is included in the estimation that poetry has obtained. I wonder whether in the Beechwood grounds yesterday, listening to the poet's music chanted by a voice that would dwell lovingly and eloquently on every tender chord, my sweet sister tasted any of that 'honey-dew of life,' which she thinks it her duty, and perhaps her appointed destiny, to leave to such as Lizzie Vivian."

Why Lizzie Vivian, unless the honey-dew she spoke of was associated in her secret thoughts with Lizzie's friend?

I hastened, on Gertrude's departure, to conclude my dressing, and soon followed her down stairs, intending, by extra kindness and affection, to atone for the teasing I had inflicted on her, and which I was sure she resented, not understanding that beneath it all lay a deep, deep interest in her happiness and peace of mind.

I found my mother alone, bending with a very distressed countenance over a letter she held open in her hands.

"Come here, Ethel," she said, the moment I was in the room; "the children won't be down just yet, and I must have you read this —from Mrs. Vivian. It has given me a dreadful shock, and made me feel quite ill. I saw your sister cross the lawn a minute ago, but I had not even the strength to call her in. Sit down, my

love, and read it at once, and tell me
what we can do."

I took the letter without sitting down, and
read as follows :—

" My Dear Madam,—

"It grieves me deeply to
have to inform you that the conduct of your
relative, Madlle. Kauffman, has been for
some little time less satisfactory than I
could have wished, considering that three of
my dear children have been entrusted wholly
to her care. I have, however, been slow to
suspect, still slower to condemn—the young
lady suited me as a governess, and I was very
unwilling to contemplate the idea of dismiss-
ing her. At present I have no choice in the
matter, since things have reached a climax
which necessitates immediate action on my
part. All details of this, to me, most distressing
affair, I will leave for Madlle. Kauffman to
communicate to you, as she will probably

arrive at Graybourne a few hours after this
letter. Trusting that your daughters continue
to be satisfied with Lizzie's industry and
progress, and adding my very kind regards
to them,

"I remain, dear Madam,

"Yours very truly,

"SUSAN VIVIAN."

A strong feeling of shame, of reflected
degradation, had been burning at my heart as
I read Mrs. Vivian's letter. This girl was
our cousin, our near relative, and whatever
disgrace might attach to her, we must in some
measure share. I had never till now experienced any sensation of the kind; it was
new, and altogether painful to me; not the
less so on account of the circumstances in
which I was myself placed as the affianced
wife of a clergyman. But after the first
stinging emotion had passed, I remembered
that my mother was likely to feel the matter,

on Guy's account, even more bitterly than I
did.   I gave the letter back into her hands,
and sat down beside her.

"Well, Ethel, what do you think of it?
What does it mean ?   What can poor foolish
Meta have been doing ?"

Then I repeated to mamma all the gossip
I had heard from Mrs. Arnott, and added my
opinion that this was what Meta had been
doing.   Gertie came in before my story was
finished, and we discussed the whole affair
very sadly and seriously, till breakfast and
the pupils obliged us to discontinue it.
Mamma was completely upset, and could
not swallow a mouthful.   I knew what was
in her thoughts, but I had no means of com-
forting her.

When we were alone again she re-perused
the unfortunate letter—(how many persons
there are who will read and re-read, though
they may know by heart the written words
that have strongly affected them, in the hope

it would appear that each new reading may throw some additional light upon the matter); and having once more reached the end, she looked up and groaned, rather than said:—

"Oh, my poor, poor Guy! how will he bear it?"

"Surely," exclaimed Gertrude, warmly, "when Guy discovers that his idol is only made of very common and inferior clay, he will have no difficulty in foregoing his infatuated worship. Since Meta is unworthy, I think it just as well that she should have come out in her true character before Guy could be brought under her influence again."

"But we are forgetting," I said, "that Guy is not even the most to be pitied in this wretched case, supposing Mrs. Vivian's letter and Mrs. Arnott's news have really a correspondence. There is poor Alicia Clarkson whose whole life will have been blighted—to say nothing of Edmund's mother, who is not likely easily to forgive or look over any dishonourable conduct on the part of her son.''

I did not deem it necessary at present to communicate what Mr. Wyke had revealed to me about the living heir of the earldom of Clinton, but I wanted, by drawing attention to Alicia and Mrs. Hallam, to turn my mother's thoughts—at any rate for a little while— from her own son, and the despair she foresaw for him.

By-and-bye, when the bell rang, Gertrude went up-stairs to the school-room, entreating me in a whisper to stay with mamma and let her talk out all her thoughts on the subject that was harassing them. We could not tell how soon Meta might arrive, and the position we should assume towards her ought certainly to be settled beforehand.

" This is a sad cloud on your bright and happy prospects, my Ethel," mamma ob-

served, kindly, when my sister was gone. " I wrote to Guy yesterday, telling him all about you and Mr. Wyke. I little thought my next letter would convey to him tidings of such a different nature. I hope," (with a sudden look of alarm as if the idea had that moment struck her), " I hope the vicar will not allow this unfortunate affair to alter his sentiments towards you. He was very fond of Alicia, and would be sure to resent any injustice done to her. What do you think, my dear?"

" I think, mamma, that, even putting aside the question of affection, Mr. Wyke is too good a man to visit on my head the sins of a distant cousin. If Meta has disgraced us in a yet more serious way than we have at present reason to believe, I will give him up of my own accord. I would not suffer him to ally himself and his unspotted name to a family that could be pointed at."

I felt that I grew a little pale as I spoke—

as the bare possibility of relinquishing the love which had flooded all my life with sunshine, crossed my mind in a shape that was not wholly visionary. My mother looked at me till the tears came in her eyes. Then she drew me to her, and kissed me fondly.

"My dearest child, there is no fear of anything so terrible as this. Meta is quite as proud as she is vain—whatever she has done has been dictated by ambition, as we agreed just now. Mr. Wyke will see the whole matter as we see it, and I don't know why it should really even delay your marriage. We must be thinking (whatever else presses) about your wedding clothes immediately."

I was glad that the current of her thoughts had changed and taken this (under the circumstances) natural direction. For a good hour we went heart and soul into the subject of calicoes, and linens, and silks, and all the other materials employed in the fabrication of

N 5

marriage outfits, and at the end of that time, as
I was thinking I might safely leave her and go
and help Gertie up-stairs, the sound of rapidly
approaching wheels made us both turn pale
for a minute, and finally sent me flying down
the pathway to the gate, too impatient to wait
for Betsy's leisurely arrival.

Of course it was Meta. Her fair face (very
pale now and with a look of cold defiance in
it) was turned to the carriage window nearest
to me as I opened the gate and stood waiting
for the driver to draw up his horses. As
soon as this was done, I approached my
cousin and welcomed her kindly, at least, if
not affectionately. She did not offer to kiss
me, and when she spoke I fancied her voice
even colder than her look. The driver came
now and opened the carriage door, upon
which Meta sprang out, gave some directions
about her luggage, and then, taking her purse
from her pocket, began parleying with the
man about his fare.

Whilst she was thus occupied I picked up a half-torn letter which she had dragged from her pocket with the purse, and held it till she was free to receive it. Quite inadvertently my eye glanced at the signature attached to this torn and crumpled paper, as I gave it back to her. The colour mounted to both our faces as she saw what I had done, and I saw that my really unconscious *espionage* had been detected.

"It is of no consequence," said Meta, haughtily, as I began some bungling apology. "I never intended to make a secret of this matter—there is no need. But I shall prefer speaking in the presence of Mrs. Beamish, and offering to her my justification—shall we go in?"

I had just said "yes," and was standing aside for my cousin to pass through the gate before me, when the sound of my own name, spoken by a voice I was not likely to mistake, drove Meta and everything connected with her out of my mind for the moment. She, too, had turned, however, on hearing me called, had given one startled look, and then without a word had hurried away up the garden path to the house.·

"Ethel, who—who is that lady?" said Mr. Wyke, eagerly (he had not been quite so shy of looking into ladies' faces since his election of a wife was made), "who is she, and what is she doing here?"

"She is my cousin, Meta Kauffman," I replied quietly, for of course the recognition was no surprise to me; "you had better come in and be introduced to her, though I regret to say she has been sent from the Vivians in disgrace. We have had no particulars yet, but I fear Mrs. Arnott's gossip was for once reliable information. Mamma is in a dreadful way."

I don't think he heard a word of this beyond my reply to his question. His face expressed astonishment, mystification, doubt, and no inconsiderable degree of annoyance. Thus he stood for more than a minute, looking up the pathway whence Meta had but just disappeared. At length, when I was growing tired of his silence, and a little jealous of his preoccupation, he turned, and drew my arm gently within his own.

"If I am neither dreaming nor blind, Ethel," he said, "that lady is not Miss Kauffman, but Mrs. Alan Beresford. Come into the house, my darling, for you look pale, and let me make the acquaintance of this mysterious cousin of yours at last."

END OF VOL. II.

T. C. NEWBY, 30, Welbeck Street, Cavendish Square, London.

In 1 Vol., Post 8vo., Price 10s. 6d.

HEROIC IDYLS,

AND OTHER POEMS.

By WALTER SAVAGE LANDOR.

" These Idyls may take their place with those heretofore given us by Mr. Landor. Judged of simply by their merits, they compel that rare admiration which we yield only to noble ideals made palpable by true art. As recent works, they claim the tribute of our wonder no less than our delight."—*Athenæum.*

" Landor's works, stamped as they are with the impress of high and original intellect, will ensure for him a proud position among the master-minds of the period."—*Bell's Messenger.*

" The same classical feeling which has given a harmony even to the most fanciful of his 'Imaginary Conversations,' and moulded the thoughts of our English poet in the lines of Greek simplicity and beauty, is to be found here, as delicately marked as ever. Few artists of modern times have taken a larger range, or have carried out a clearly conceived purpose with a steadier hand. When Mr. Landor is gone, we shall have lost at once the founder, and almost the only follower, of a peculiar and grand school."—*Saturday Review.*

" Full of vigour and tender expressions."—*Observer.*

" Here we recognise the dignified pathos and tranquil beauty charac-teristic of the best of his 'Hellenics.' "—*Reader.*

" A book of great merit, containing many passages of singular power, grace, and freshness of style, which it would be hard to match in any modern versifiers."—*Morning Herald.*

" For simplicity, classical purity, and keen sarcasm of thought and ex-pression, Landor almost stands alone. The book is full of his wonted vigour, skill, and grace."—*Oriental Budget.*

In 1 Vol., post 8vo., price 10s. 6d.

ZEAL IN THE WORK OF THE MINISTRY,

AT L'ABBE DUBOIS.

"There is a tone of piety and reality in the work of l'Abbe Dubois, and a unity of aim, which is to fix the priest's mind on the duties and responsibilities of his whole position, and which we admire. The writer is occupied supremely with one thought of contributing to the salvation of souls and to the glory of God."—*Literary Churchman.*

"It abounds in sound and discriminating reflections and valuable hints. No portion of a Clergyman's duties is overlooked."—*The Ecclesiastic.*

"This volume enters so charmingly into the minutiæ of clerical life, that we know none so calculated to assist the young priest, and direct him in his duties. It is a precious legacy of wisdom to all the priesthood."—*Union.*

In 2 Vols., Post 8vo., Price 21s.

ANECDOTAL MEMOIRS OF ENGLISH PRINCES

By W. H. DAVENPORT ADAMS.

Author of "Memorable Battles in English History," &c.

"The author has drawn his materials from many sources; and without seeking to usurp the province of the historian, or to disturb or affirm the verdict pronounced upon the events to which he refers, or the personages who figure on the busy stage, he has given connected accounts of their general character and career, of the stirring scenes in which they each acted a prominent part, and of the times in which they lived, which will interest the general reader, and furnish landmarks for the guidance of the student."—*Morning Post.*

"There can be no doubt of these memoirs being favourably receive by the public."—*Observer.*

"Mr. Adams manifests the same tact and discretion which has made his former publications so highly interesting."—*Bell's Messenger.*

"Mr. Adams has here opened an almost inexhaustible mine of anecdotal wealth. Scattered over the pages of our history anecdotes of the doings of English Princes have hitherto been interesting only, or chiefly, in connection with the era in which the incidents occurred. Mr. Adams has shown that the anecdotes have an interest of their own, apart from historical connection."—*Morning Herald.*

In 2 Volumes, Octavo, price 21s.

ENGLISH AMERICA,

OR,

PICTURES OF CANADIAN PLACES AND PEOPLE.

EXHIBITING OUR COLONIAL POSSESSIONS ON THE AMERICAN CONTINENT
IN THEIR MORAL, SOCIAL, RELIGIOUS, PHYSICAL, MILITARY,
ECONOMICAL, AND INDUSTRIAL ASPECTS.

By SAMUEL PHILLIPS DAY,

Special Correspondent in Canada of the *Morning Herald*;

Author of "Down South; or Experiences at the Seat of War in
America," &c., &c.

THE FOURTH EDITION, ILLUSTRATED.

In 1 Vol., Post 8vo., Price 7s. 6d.

A NARRATIVE OF ADVENTURES

IN FRANCE AND FLANDERS,

DURING THE LATE WAR.

By CAPTAIN EDWARD BOYS,

ROYAL NAVY.

" Readers will like this curious narrative, which has all the charm
of truthfulness, which few writers, excepting De Foe, could have
written half so truthfully; and Captain Boys' interesting and patriotic
story is all truth in itself."—*Illustrated Times.*

"Many of the events recorded have long since become matters of
history; they are, however, so mixed up with personal adventures,
simple truth conveyed in a simple form, that we read on with un-
flagging attention."—*Morning Advertiser.*

"Every youth in Her Majesty's dominions should read these
adventures."—*Daily Post.*

FAMILY MOURNING.

MESSRS. JAY

Would respectfully announce that great saving may be made by
purchasing Mourning at their Establishment,

THEIR STOCK OF

FAMILY·MOURNING

BEING

THE LARGEST IN EUROPE.

MOURNING COSTUME

OF EVERY DESCRIPTION

KEPT READY-MADE,

And can be forwarded to Town or Country at a moment's notice.

The most reasonable Prices are charged, and the wear of every
Article Guaranteed.

THE LONDON

GENERAL MOURNING WAREHOUSE,

247 & 248, REGENT STREET,

(NEXT THE CIRCUS.)

JAY'S.

THE TEETH AND BREATH.

How often do we find the human face divine disfigured by neglecting the chiefest of its ornaments, and the breath made disagreeable to companions by non-attention to the Teeth! Though perfect in their structure and composition, to keep them in a pure and healthy state requires some little trouble; and if those who are blessed with well-formed teeth knew how soon decay steals into the mouth, making unsightly what otherwise are delightful to admire, and designating unhealthiness by the impurity of the breath, they would spare no expense to chase away these fatal blemishes. But although most ladies are careful, and even particular in these delicate matters, yet few are sufficiently aware of the imperative necessity of avoiding all noxious and mineral substances of an acrid nature, and of which the greater part of the cheap tooth-powders and pastes of the present day are composed. It is highly satisfactory to point out Messrs. ROWLANDS' ODONTO, or Pearl Dentifrice, as a preparation free from all injurious elements, and eminently calculated to embellish and preserve the dental structure, to impart a grateful fragrance to the breath, and to embellish and perpetuate the graces of the mouth – *Court Journal.*

ROWLANDS' ODONTO

Is a White Powder, compounded of the choicest and most recherché ingredients of the oriental herbal, of inestimable value in preserving and beautifying the teeth, strengthening the gums, and in giving a pleasing fragrance to the breath. Price 2s. 9d per box. – Sold by Chemists and Perfumers.

. Ask for "ROWLANDS' ODONTO."

THE HUMAN HAIR.

Of the numerous compounds constantly announced for promoting the growth or reproduction of the Human Hair, few survive even in name, beyond a very limited period; whilst

ROWLANDS' MACASSAR OIL,

with a reputation unparalleled, is still on the increase in public estimation. The unprecedented success of this discovery, either in preserving the hair in its original strength and beauty, or restoring it when lost, is universally known and appreciated, and is certified by numerous testimonials and by the highest authorities. It has obtained the patronage of Royalty, not only of our own Court, but those of the whole of Europe From its exquisite purity and delicacy, it is admirably adapted for the hair of children, even of the most tender age, and is in constant use in the nursery of Royalty, and by the families of the Nobility and Aristocracy. It is alike suited for either sex; and, whether employed to embellish the tresses of female beauty, or to add to the attractions of manly grace, will be found an indispensable auxiliary to the toilet both of ladies and gentlemen —Price 3s. 6d. and 7s.; or family bottles (equal to four small) at 10s. 6d., and double that size, 21s. – Sold by all Chemists and Perfumers.

. Ask for "ROWLANDS' MACASSAR OIL."

EMULATION, in whatever pursuit, where general utility is the object kept in view, is one of the immutable privileges of Genius; but it requires no slight degree of perspicuous attention to distinguish Originality from Imitation, and the exercise of Caution becomes of more than usual importance, where the effect of a remedial application (both as regards health and personal appearance), is the subject of consideration; these observations are imperatively called for from A. ROWLAND & SONS, of London, whose successful introduction of several articles of acknowledged and standard excellence for the Toilet has given rise to fertility of imitation, perfectly unprecedented: they would have deemed observation unnecessary were temporary deceptions unaccompanied by permanently injurious effects—it is with reference to ROWLANDS' KALYDOR *for the Complexion*, that the Public are particularly interested in the present remarks. This preparation eminently *balsamic, restorative*, and *invigorating :*—the result of scientific botanical research, and equally celebrated for safety in application, as for unfailing efficacy in *removing all Impurities and Discolorations of the skin*, has its "Spurious Imitations of the most deleterious character," containing mineral astringents utterly ruinous to the Complexion, and, by their repellant action endangering health, which render it indispensably necessary to see that the words "ROWLANDS' KALYDOR" are on the wrapper, with the signature in red ink, "*A. Rowland & Sons.*" Sold by Chemists and Perfumers.

BEDSTEADS, BEDDING, AND BED ROOM FURNITURE.

HEAL & SON'S

Show Rooms contain a large assortment of Brass Bedsteads, suitable both for home use and for Tropical Climates.

Handsome Iron Bedsteads, with Brass Mountings, and elegantly Japanned.

Plain Iron Bedsteads for Servants.

Every description of Woodstead, in Mahogany, Birch, and Walnut Tree Woods, Polished Deal and Japanned, all fitted with Beding and Furnitures complete.

Also, every description of Bed Room Furniture, consisting of Wardrobes, Chests of Drawers, Washstands, Tables, Chairs, Sofas, Couches, and every article for the complete furnishing of a Bed Room.

AN

ILLUSTRATED CATALOGUE,

Containing Designs and Prices of 150 articles of Bed Room Furniture, as well as of 100 Bedsteads, and Prices of every description of Bedding

Sent Free by Post.

HEAL & SON,

BEDSTEAD, BEDDING,

AND

BED ROOM FURNITURE MANUFACTURERS,

196, TOTTENHAM COURT ROAD,

LONDON. W.